THE TENDER FLAME

THE TENDER FLAME

Anne Saunders

Chivers Press • Thorndike Press
Bath, England   Waterville, Maine USA

This Large Print edition is published by Chivers Press, England, and by Thorndike Press, USA.

Published in 2003 in the U.K. by arrangement with Margaret Barry.

Published in 2003 in the U.S. by arrangement with Juliet Burton Literary Agency.

U.K. Hardcover ISBN 0–7540–8930–4 (Chivers Large Print)
U.K. Softcover   ISBN 0–7540–8931–2 (Camden Large Print)
U.S. Softcover   ISBN 0–7862–5123–9 (Nightingale Series)

The text of this Large Print edition is unabridged.
Other aspects of the book may vary from the original edition.

Set in 16 pt. New Times Roman.

Printed in Great Britain on acid-free paper.

British Library Cataloguing in Publication Data available

Library of Congress Cataloging-in-Publication Data

Saunders, Anne.
    The tender flame / by Anne Saunders.
      p. cm.
   ISBN 0–7862–5123–9 (lg. print : sc : alk. paper)
    1. Single fathers—Fiction. 2. Nannies—Fiction 3. Large type books. I. Title.
PR6069.A88T46 2003
813'.54—dc21   2002044727

CHAPTER ONE

It was decision time again for Jan. Annabel Spedding, her employer, had died unexpectedly. Any day now, Annabel's husband, David Spedding, would turn up with instructions for her. Until then, Jan could remain at the cottage to look after Stephanie, Annabel's four year old daughter.

Jan, a copper-knob with hazel eyes, was fortunately blessed with an easy going temperament. Recent events, because she had coped with Annabel single-handed, had proved that she was sensible and level-headed in a crisis. She was also a caring sort of girl who could raise a spirited temper when she sensed injustice. Well-liked herself, there was only one person she actively disliked, and that was David Spedding, her late employer's husband. The fact that she had never met him was irrelevant. When his wife and daughter had needed him most, he hadn't been there.

Jan had applied for the job in this rather remote and lovely part of Yorkshire to get away from a man by the name of Martin Groves. While she hadn't entirely forgotten Martin, she remembered him in a different way, so you could say the experiment had worked. She couldn't possibly have known she would be escaping one problem merely to land

1

herself in another.

When David Spedding turned up would he dismiss her on the spot, or would he ask her to stay on to look after Stephanie? Could she work for a man she had no respect for and looked upon with contempt? Her affection for the child provided the answer to that. She must. For Stephanie's sake she must swallow her scruples and, if necessary, fight to stay.

Last time she had reached a crossroad situation—when Martin had dropped her for someone else—she had been knocked off balance. This time . . . it was difficult to peel away the numbness to assess her true feelings. The sudden, unexpected death of Annabel Spedding had brought her up against hard reality with a jolt. She grieved at a comparatively young life being snuffed out as effortlessly as a candle, even though she never got to know her as she should have done. She had eaten, slept, worked, and spent her leisure hours under the same tiny roof as her employer, but she had never got close to her. Now that Annabel was dead, she wished she had. She didn't weep because she had lost a dearly loved friend, but because she hadn't.

Annabel had been too young to die. And her small daughter, four-year-old Stephanie, was too young to be caught up in the tragic tangle of it all. Stephanie was the one who mattered now. Stephanie was the only consideration. It must all, somehow, be put

2

behind her. For a while the child would be bruised, that was inevitable, but she must not be allowed to carry the type of scar that would mar her sunny temperament for the rest of her life. Perhaps it was no more than a comforting myth at that, but Jan believed she could help to preserve the little girl's happy serenity.

Blessed of parents who were devoted to each other, her own childhood had known no such torment or trauma. During her formative years the illusion had held steady that the world was a fun playground, and if she had ever stopped to think about it, she would have held firm to the conviction that she was going to skip through schooldays and walk on through adult life with a charmed step. She hadn't stopped to think about it because it was something that was and would always be.

At school she had been a popular girl, not a brilliant scholar, but industrious enough to get by. She was a plodder. Not like Martin who'd worn the tag of lazy genius. He was the tall, good-looking son of 'Aunt' Dora. 'Aunt' was the courtesy title she gave to her mother's best friend. As a smitten schoolgirl she had looked at Martin with adoration in her eyes. The first time he asked her for a date she almost died on the spot from an overdose of pure delight. Wow! She couldn't believe her luck. She took hours to get ready, selecting and discarding until she got it right. To look as though you've casually thrown on a few things is the most time-consuming look to achieve. Her efforts paid off and Martin told her she was pretty. Unfortunately she blushed a fiery red and couldn't think of a thing to say. For an hour and a half!

That's it, she thought. A boy who could have his pick isn't going to waste his time on a struck-dumb idiot like me. He'll never ask me out again.

But he had. He'd asked her out so many times that their names became inseparable. Jan-and-Martin. When party time came round it was unheard of to invite one without the other. They were the perfect pair, as right as coffee and cream. She was the coffee, the stability in the partnership. Martin was the luxury cream topping.

When did the cream start to sour? Should she have known that Martin was beginning to tire of her? Weren't there supposed to be unmistakable signs? Was she so smug and happy that she failed to notice that their friendship had a hollow core? Without a solid centre it was doomed from the beginning and eventual collapse was inevitable.

Sylvia Friers, a so-called friend who had wanted Martin for herself and had never forgiven Jan for getting him, whispered maliciously in her ear that he was seeing another girl on the quiet. A girl with round moon eyes, silver blonde hair, and a gentle, ethereal beauty that was almost mystic. Her name was Tara Smith and while Jan was consumed with jealousy, her mind was surprisingly free of bitterness as she acknowledged that if it were true, Martin had improved on her. Jan wisely did not act on the warning. Alone, it did not merit positive steps being taken. She waited, watched, her mind on the alert. Was the unexpected, extravagant gift of a mid-week bouquet of flowers, when it wasn't her birthday or a day marking something special like the anniversary of their first date, a sop to his guilt for too much inattentiveness, too many broken dates? Or was it his way of saying, 'I've been a naughty boy. I strayed. But I've learnt my lesson and I'm back for good now.'?

The only way Jan could be sure which of these applied was to ask him outright. And she couldn't do that. Couldn't she? Why couldn't she?

Perhaps it wasn't the best style in the world to ask, but it was honest, and whatever else was missing between them, it wasn't honesty.

'Do you want to call it a day, Martin? If there's someone else, I'll understand.' For his sake she had kept the silly hope out of her eyes, but when she saw the relief flood into his she was glad for her own pride's sake.

Very gently he had taken her hands. 'I think I'm the biggest fool in creation, but yes I do. Because yes there is.'

She had wished him all the luck in the

world, and even managed to aim a goodbye kiss at his cheek. So far so good. But then she turned coward. Much as it would pain her to leave her happy home, she had to get away. Her heart pleaded for it not to be so far away that she couldn't hop on a bus or a train for dutiful daughterly visits home. Her head knew it must be as far away as possible to abolish the risk of bumping into Martin and Tara until such times as she did not go weak with longing for a glimpse of blue eyes with back-curling lashes, straw-coloured hair and a lopsided grin. She wouldn't need to pack a photo of Martin in her suitcase when she left. His face was too bright in her mind to fade in a hurry.

She scoured the adverts in the situations vacant columns of every newspaper she could lay her hands on, and this one caught her eye. Wanted: Pleasantly disposed female to care for disabled young woman and daughter. Expected to live in. Nursing experience is not essential. A sense of humour is.

Jan had phoned to apply for the job one day, attended the interview the next day, and before the week was out she found herself installed at Larkspur Cottage in Willowbridge which, at two hundred miles from her home town, was just the right distance away.

It was a snowdrop sweet, Winter-crisp day with baby drifts of snow cradled in unexpected nooks and crannies, and although she was staggering at the speed with which her life had changed course, she had found her new surroundings delightful.

Grey-stone cottages haphazardly climbed the hillside to curl round the fourteenth century church. The main essential shops, Johnson the butcher, Beevers the baker, and Spink the post office and general purpose store, were all family concerns that had been handed down from generation to generation. Even the newcomer, Studio Pottery, had been trading since 1951. It was a tightly loyal, fiercely feuding little community. These plain-speaking people were as honest as the carbolic soap sold over Alice Spink's counter. Even in awe of them, Jan genuinely liked them, and was touched when, in their blunt way, they made it known that they were willing to give her a try.

Never would she forget her first sight of her employer. Annabel Spedding, a striking figure in a wheelchair, had waist-length black hair, cornflower blue eyes, and a face of riveting beauty. Jan believed Annabel's claim that the boys used to go mad to take her out. With an amused, almost smug quirk in her eye she had confided that her marriage to David Spedding had caused quite a furore. He was the one least likely tipped to get her to the altar.

Tragedy had struck on their wedding day. They were being driven to the reception by a friend, when the car met with an accident. Annabel had given this information to Jan starkly and without any softening frills. The driver of the car, Stephen Grant, had died instantly and Annabel's life had hung on a thread.

'For a while it looked as though I would lose my baby.' So saying, her lovely eyes had lifted to Jan's, daring her to register surprise.

Jan had kept a non-committal face, thinking it was quaint of Annabel if she expected her to be shocked. Jan got the strangest feeling it was something more than that, something deeper. A wild sort of defiance crossed Annabel's expression, at odds with the heart-tugging sadness of her smile.

'Nobody lifted a scandalised eyebrow or made a single derogatory or harsh comment when it leaked out that a baby was on the way.'

'Why should they?' Jan had challenged. Even if times hadn't changed, any normal, caring person would think that Annabel had been punished enough.

From her own observations, Jan knew that local feeling was warm towards Annabel. Everyone admired her for her courage. It took guts to tilt a chin at adversity. Instead of shrinking into herself she had been arrogant in her determination to live. Live, not exist as a pathetic figure in a wheelchair. Only Annabel could have used her chair to advantage, sitting as daintily as a queen, presiding over events, loving the fuss and attention that was lavished on her. Even Louisa Grant, who was considered to be Willowbridge's first lady and lived in the Manor House, paid court to Annabel and made a lot of Stephanie.

Some did say, though, it wasn't for love of Annabel that Stephanie was sought out for favours and attention. Wasn't it her son Stephen's careless driving that crashed the car? This fact was given to Jan in whisper-soft tones. Stephen Grant had failed to earn himself the respect and affection that was given to his mother, but he had paid for his folly with his life and it wasn't done to talk ill of the dead. Tongues were more lively, less charitable, and not locked by superstitious fears when it came to Annabel's husband, David Spedding. It was said the moment he knew the extent of her injuries, he took off as if the devil was at his heels. Desertion, they called it. Cruel, inhuman desertion.

In the six months Jan had been there he'd never visited. In view of this it was perhaps foolish of her, but she sometimes wondered if he was as unfeeling as local opinion made out. The cottage was his and he paid all the bills. Jan had been shocked at Annabel's free spending and the careless way she ran up accounts. It was a wonder the poor man could hold his head above water.

Ralph Goodall, Willowbridge's only solicitor and the man in charge of Annabel's affairs, had instructed Jan to put the outstanding bills to one side until he could contact the husband. This he had done and David Spedding was presumably on his way home, unfortunately too late to attend Annabel's funeral which had taken place two weeks ago. It made Jan realise that her earlier sympathies had been misplaced. What sort of person must he be? She couldn't go on making excuses for a man who hadn't made the effort to be at his wife's funeral to pay his last respects. Apart from the common decency angle, he should have wanted to be there for Stephanie's sake. Stephanie had needed a father's comfort.

Jan's own determination had strengthened. Come what may, she wasn't going to add to Stephanie's heartbreak by walking out on her, even though staying on presented difficulties.

Annabel had been dilatory in all respects where money was concerned. Jan hadn't received remuneration for several weeks. She didn't like to ask the solicitor for her back-wages, but without money she couldn't buy food. She supposed she could have copied Annabel and run up a bill, but she felt there were enough of these to present to David Spedding as it was, without adding more.

She had made quite searching enquiries about getting a job locally. Something part-time because Stephanie mustn't feel that she was being neglected, which brought in just enough ready cash to tide them over until Stephanie's errant father put in an appearance. Everyone was sympathetic, but there was nothing suitable to be had. Of course, she hadn't made her financial difficulties known, and it was thought she was suffering from a time-on-her-hands malaise.

The grandmother clock chimed a reminder that it was nearing the hour to collect Stephanie from play-school. If she wasn't among the first three to be collected, she created. Since her mother's death she needed constant reassurance that someone was always on hand. Even with all Jan's vigilance she had gone back to the babyish habit of sucking her thumb.

Sighing on feelings of helplessness and frustration—because what more could she do?—Jan dusted a powder-puff over her nose, smoothed a coral-pink lipstick across her mouth, which was about the most attention her face ever got. Her complexion had the quality of fine porcelain. Her nose was slightly pert, her chin small but determined. Unspectacular she thought. As though by token of apology, nature had endowed her with memorably large hazel eyes which were colour-linked to her mood. Predominantly green when she was in a good mood, lightening to gold when she was predisposed to laughter, but darkening to stormy brown at the first hint of temper. Her hair, inherited from Grandmother Ashton who had the reputation of being a firebrand, was a rich chestnut brown veering to red. Her

11

crowning glory had earned her the nickname of Copper Knob at school. Grandmother Ashton was a flamboyant enough character to carry her distinctive hair colouring, Jan felt that she wasn't.

She was barely a quarter way down the hill when a splash of rain on her nose drew her attention to the glowering sky. It was black, in a daytime way, and it would have been sensible to go back for protective clothing, but optimistically she hoped it would blow over. It didn't. By the time she got to the square where the market traders were hastily packing up, she was squelching with every step she took.

Most of the refugees from the storm had packed into the Coffee Bean. It was the only place offering shelter that would give Jan a clear view of the play-school building, so she reluctantly followed suit. In her present financial straits she begrudged paying out for a cup of coffee; on the other hand she couldn't afford to stay out in the downpour and risk catching a chill. As it was there was a tickle in her nose that erupted ominously into a sneeze.

The Coffee Bean was always well attended on market days, but today it was bulging at the seams. Jan made her way towards the only vacant chair and sat down at a table already occupied by a man with dark hair, nicely cut, and a slightly averted face. Her profile impression of him was of a good strong nose and chin, offset by high cheekbones and a mouth that was too sensitive to be permanently clamped in such an awesomely straight line.

Jan had a tendency to reverse the proper order of things. It was typical of her to sit down first, and then ask permission to do so.

'Excuse me, but is it all right for me to sit here?'

'Yes, please do,' he said, vaguely waving her down before he'd properly turned to look at her. 'Ah! I see that you are already seated.'

The side view of him had given the impression of strength and power. It hadn't prepared her for the dynamic effect of being the subject of his amused scrutiny. 'M'm. You're very wet.'

She agreed that she was, and her hands did something completely out of character. They lifted fussily to her hair, as if her fingers could magic the flattened, sorry little strands into some semblance of order.

He was attractive enough to be familiar with this kind of feminine response. The salacious twinkle in his eye confirmed this. But it was the quirk softening of his mouth that told Jan this same reaction in a damp mouse took him by surprise. He seemed to like damp mice.

'The waitress doesn't appear to be coming to take your order,' he observed kindly.

'No,' Jan agreed, thankful for once she wasn't the type to inspire quick service. With a bit of luck the waitress wouldn't spot her before it was time to walk across the road to collect Stephanie, and she could have a warm through and a dry out without it having to cost her anything.

He snapped his fingers above her head, and wouldn't you just know it, a waitress came at the double.

'Sorry to keep you waiting. What was it?'

'Coffee, please,' Jan said resignedly.

'A cup or a pot?'

'A pot,' Awesome Mouth who was soon to be renicknamed Busybody answered for her. 'And some hot buttered toast and a selection of cakes.'

'Really!' Jan said when the waitress had gone. 'I'm capable of answering for myself. You shouldn't have ordered the toast and cakes because I'm not hungry.'

'Then it's morally wrong of you to go about looking as though you could do to wrap yourself round a huge steak.'

'You could add all the trimmings and a mountain of chips and I'd still look like this. Can I help it if I'm naturally skinny?'

'Slender sounds nicer,' he admonished. 'If you haven't been dieting, and I'll take your word for it that you haven't, then it must be the other. He's not worth it, you know.'

'Who isn't?' she queried, looking perplexed.

'The man who walked out on you.'

'I got over him months ago,' she said ingenuously and with belated regret, because

14

she didn't have to advertise the fact that Martin had walked out on her. 'This man didn't walk out on *me.*'

That slipped out without thinking. She had had David Spedding in mind when she said it, but the last thing she intended to do was gossip about him to a stranger.

'The inference being that he walked out on someone?' he said with uncanny perception.

This time Jan thought before she replied. For the last few moments she had been trying to work out who he might be. Strangers weren't uncommon in Willowbridge, which was pretty enough to attract tourists. But tourists came in youthful-looking twosomes kitted out in jeans with haversacks on their backs, or they tumbled out of cars in family groups, Mum, Dad, offspring, sometimes Gran and Grandfather, and quite often with the family pet in tow. A man on his own might be here for market day, but he would definitely be of farming stock, and Awesome Mouth had a citified look about him. Two other possibilities still remained. Mrs. Grant, *the* Mrs. Grant of the Manor House, was reputedly interested in selling some valuable porcelain and an oriental painting in ink on silk, and it was said she had invited a dealer over to appraise them and give her a price. Awesome Mouth might be the dealer. The remaining possibility was quite balking. He could be David Spedding.

Afterwards, if someone had asked Jan why

15

she did it she would have had to admit she didn't know. There was a feeling of revenge in gossiping about David Spedding to a stranger. She could hit back at him for Annabel, safe in the knowledge that the parties concerned meant nothing to him and the talk wouldn't stay in his mind to be repeated all over Willowbridge, as it would have been if she'd aired her views to one of its inmates. Indeed, in a few hours he would have departed, probably for ever. On the other hand, if the stranger turned out to be David Spedding, never would she have a better opportunity of telling him a few home truths than this moment while she was still unaware of his identity.

She took a deep breath and said: 'He walked out on his wife and child, would you believe?'

He replied unperturbably, with just a cynical lift of one eyebrow: 'Quite easily. There are some despicable characters in this world.'

On reflection, Jan wasn't certain whether the eyebrow action was cynical, or if he was teasing her naïveté. If this latter was his intent, it served its purpose. It goaded her to further indiscretion.

'You can say that again! This one didn't even come back to attend his wife's funeral.'

He was Awesome Mouth again with a vengeance. He said bitingly: 'Perhaps he had a reason.'

Funnily enough, this is what Jan had said in his defence in the face of local condemnation. It was a relief to voice the disapproval she'd had to keep bottled up. 'I've tried to be charitable about this, but I can't. There isn't a reason that will stand up to his non-appearance on that day.' And now she wasn't hitting back in revenge any more, she was having a reaction. She'd had to be brave for Stephanie's sake, but the truth was she'd never dwelt at such close quarters with death before. Her beloved grandmother had been very ill once, and near to death, but unlike Annabel she had recovered.

Jan had been with Annabel, looked after her, had barely let go of her hand during her last hours. At the same time she'd had to keep a bright face for Stephanie's sake. In Stephanie's eyes she represented grown-up calmness and authority. But she didn't feel grown-up or calm. She felt very young, very insecure; she needed someone to come along and take command of the whole horrible situation. She wanted to object to the role that had been forced upon her. She wanted to scream and shout. She wanted strong arms to hold her, and a strong shoulder upon which to sob out her fear and frustration. She needed to lash out at the man who hadn't been there to shoulder his responsibility.

'He's callous and heartless,' she said with deep feeling that verged on hate.

17

She heard the stranger's sharp intake of breath, but she was too incensed to react to it. 'I know the crash wasn't his fault in that his hand wasn't on the steering wheel, but if Annabel hadn't married him in the first place she wouldn't have been in the car at that particular moment, so that makes him indirectly responsible for her terrible injuries which chained her to a wheelchair.' She had said *his* fault, but she might as well have said *your* fault, because she knew he was David Spedding.

He said: 'Go on.' Something she had every intention of doing because she had vaulted the barriers of commonsense and was past heeding the tone of his voice.

In the circumstances it was silly of her to say: 'You can't know—' Of course he knew—'and I shouldn't be telling you all this—' That was rich, hysterically rich—'but as a result of the crash which happened as they were on their way from the church to the wedding reception, Annabel was severely crippled. Not that I ever heard her utter one word of blame against him.' She couldn't resist getting that dig in. 'She was marvellous. Brave right up to the end, which was two weeks ago. And he—' Her voice choked on emotion—'that husband of hers didn't think enough about her to come to her funeral. You would have thought he'd come, wouldn't you, if only to comfort his little girl?'

'You are right about one thing.' And now Awesome Mouth awesomely surpassed the name she had given him. 'You shouldn't be telling me all this. Do you always gossip so indiscriminately to strangers, Miss Ashton?'

She could have tossed back her head and retorted, 'But you aren't a stranger, are you?' Instead she feigned surprise, because of course Annabel's husband would know the name of the person who was looking after his child. 'How do you know my name?'

Before he could answer, the waitress arrived with the coffee tray.

'Allow me,' he said, reaching for the coffee pot.

She was glad he took the task upon himself because her shaking fingers would have disgraced her. She thought that she was lucky he didn't pour the coffee over her head. She could no longer hope that by some miracle he would turn out to be the dealer here to see Mrs. Grant about the sale of her possessions. The dealer would have no cause to know her name.

What had she done? How could she have been so foolish? If only she had stopped to think exactly where her folly would lead. She had deliberately antagonised the man she hoped to soft-talk into letting her stay to look after Stephanie.

'I've just come from Ralph's office. He said that Annabel had engaged the services of a

19

young woman who would fit your description. He said if I hung around I'd be likely to meet up with you as it was your time to fetch Stephanie from school.' He broke off to ask: 'Isn't she a little on the young side to be going to school?'

'It's play-school, not proper school with lessons and things. It's good for her to mix with other children, and while her mother was ill it was a godsend to have her out of the house for a few hours each day.'

'Of course.' His face was a mask. 'You're not eating.'

She looked at the toast and cakes the waitress had brought with the coffee. She was too choked to eat. 'I'm sorry. I'm really not hungry. But thank you for your solicitude.'

He snorted. 'Don't fool yourself. I'm thinking of myself. I don't want you to pass out on me.'

Jan's stomach fluttered. Breakfast was a meal she frequently skipped without mishap, and today she'd been too busy mulling over her problems to bother about lunch. The error of her ways showed in her white face. She suddenly felt herself keeling over.

She didn't properly blank out, it was as if a wave of weakness had washed over her, and as she would have fallen off her chair she was aware that he reached out to grab hold of her.

'Nicely fielded,' she said with a feeble flash of humour.

An answering smile warmed his eye for the briefest moment before it slid behind a crust of ice. 'This is ridiculous. Looking after Stephanie is a job for a woman. What was Annabel thinking of when she engaged you? You are little more than a child yourself. Just how old are you?'

At the interview that was something Annabel hadn't asked. She hadn't bothered to ask much at all, and Jan hadn't volunteered the fact that she was twenty. Anyway, twenty wasn't all that young, but he would think it was. She decided to tag on a year or two, and ended up making it four.

'I'm twenty-four,' she said.

His eyes flicked over her in mocking disbelief. 'That makes it worse. A *mature* woman of twenty-four acting like an irresponsible child! Why are you shaking?' he asked abruptly. 'Are you frightened of me?'

She was terrified of him, but she could answer truthfully: 'I'm shaking because I'm very wet and very c-cold. I'm so wet I don't seem to be drying out.'

'M'm, yes. Let's fetch Stephanie out of that school and get you home and into some dry clothes. What possessed you to come out wearing only a dress and sandals in this downpour?'

'Obviously,' she said grittily, 'it wasn't raining when I set off. It didn't even *look* like rain.'

21

'Nonsense! It's looked like rain all day. Are you going to carry on arguing in this stupid fashion and risk getting a chill, or will you be sensible and do as I say?'

His hand was already raised to alert the waitress who came hurrying over with the bill. As he handed the money over to the girl, Jan noticed he could smile quite charmingly when he chose. But when his eyes came back to her they were dark and icy again. She had a queasy notion that no way could she talk herself back into the job she so desperately wanted to keep.

Of course, he hadn't actually said he was David Spedding. She was straw-grasping again. It wasn't impossible for him to be a distant relative of Annabel's who had only just got news of her death, someone who would be equally familiar with the names and the set-up, but with her luck it was most improbable. There was little doubt in her mind that he was Annabel's errant husband.

'You are . . . aren't you?' she said.

'Aren't I what?'

'Annabel's husband?'

He didn't answer, presumably because they were crossing the road to get to the long low building where play-school was held, and he was keeping his eye on the oncoming car.

He had taken her arm to guide her across, and the sensual shock of his touch stole her breath away in the most weird fashion. Her reaction was instant and hostile. She shrugged free of his grasp and challenged haughtily: 'You are David Spedding, aren't you?'

They had gained the pavement, and now his prompt reply cut through the last lingering wisp of hope. 'Yes, I'm David Spedding,' he said.

As he looked at her, Jan had the strangest feeling that he was asking for her forbearance and understanding.

But almost immediately he shattered the illusion by querying crisply: 'What's the drill?'

'We go in at this door and we are supposed to wait in the cloakroom. Listen! It sounds as though the class is still in session. Yes, look!' Peering through the glass partition at the teacher, book on knee, in the centre of a semi-circle of entranced little faces. 'There's Stephanie.'

'Where? Which one?'

After that, what more was there to understand? He didn't know his own child. And there was something sadder and infinitely more bitter to swallow. Stephanie wouldn't know him.

It wrung Jan's heart to have to answer the query in the child's upturned eyes as, the moment class was dismissed, she came running up to them.

'Look who's here, Stephanie. It's your daddy.'

Swallowing roughly, almost blinded by a sudden rush of tears, Jan was on tenterhooks as she waited to hear what the little girl would say.

The simplicity of a child's acceptance is a wonderful thing.

'Have you brought me any sweeties?' Stephanie asked.

'I just might have some in my suitcase,' he replied after a long pause.

Jan frowned at the look of struggle on his face. At the same time her throat filled as she witnessed his tender regard of the little girl. How could she equate this obviously caring man with the black villain who had deserted his wife and daughter, and had not bothered to get here for his wife's funeral?

She shook her head, but the muzziness wouldn't clear. As though from along way off she heard David say: 'My car is parked in the square.'

His hand on her elbow commanded her feet to walk. This time instead of wriggling free of his hold, she was grateful for the strength it provided.

'Are you all right, Miss Ashton?'

What a ridiculous question to ask. Of course she wasn't all right. She wished she'd taken notice of him and eaten something in the café. She wished she'd eaten some lunch. She wished she didn't feel so cold and shivery. She hoped she wasn't going down with a chill.

'I'm fine, thank you,' she said, clamping down on the strange little stirring of warmth that he should care enough about her well-being to ask, before he effectively did it for her.

As before, it was not solicitude that had motivated his enquiry. With disconcerting coolness he said: 'Then will you please pay attention. I've asked you twice to get in the car, and then we can be on our way.'

'Sorry.'

She scrambled in beside Stephanie who was already installed on the ample front seat. The little girl, who was beaming happily, had taken to David with a naturalness that was mind-boggling. Yet why Jan should be surprised by this, she didn't know. She had been preparing Stephanie to expect her father ever since Ralph, the solicitor, had dropped the word in her ear.

'There! Quite comfortable? Not too squashed?'

She stretched her legs out under the bonnet in a demonstrative way. 'I've plenty of room, thank you.'

David had spoken to her as though she were Stephanie's age, which wouldn't have been too bad if he'd chosen to look at her the way he looked at Stephanie.

And where did that alien thought spring from? She disliked David Spedding and all the cruel, callous things he stood for. If her hatred of him had lost its kick it was because she was feeling under the weather. She couldn't expect her thoughts to maintain their strength when she felt so weak. If she'd been on top form she wouldn't have been taken in by that perplexed yet tender little smile that played about his mouth when he looked at Stephanie. It was probably no more than conscience qualms. But that was odd in itself, because she hadn't credited him with having a conscience. The feeling she'd had of being in sympathy with him had no proper substance, and if ever it returned she'd do well to blow it right out of her head again.

If she was ever in danger of softening, it wouldn't hurt to remember that by his own actions David Spedding had presented a cast-iron case for resentment. A cunning person can tender up a bad look to make it look like a good look, but actions aren't prone to camouflage and speak for themselves.

There was something else, of a more basic nature, that she should have remembered but didn't.

David slid the key in the ignition, but paused before switching on. 'Just a thought. There is food in the house?'

Jan's look of dismay served as answer.

'I thought as much.'

'I can rustle up plenty of eggs for an omelet and there's . . .'

'I want a meal, not a snack. I won't be long.'

He got out of the car and marched across the road to the string of shops. He returned, in due time, with two carrier bags which he placed on the back seat.

'The natives were curious, and friendly. It could be,' he said with a mischievous, mocking glint in his eye, 'that they were friendly because I didn't feed their curiosity. I didn't introduce myself.' He then asked in a gravely speculative voice: 'Am I right in thinking that if I'd told them who I was, I would have got a very different reaction?'

Jan was taken aback. Could he be serious? 'Do you need to ask that?'

'Not any more,' he said soberly. 'Your face has supplied the answer. So everybody shares your unfavourable opinion of me. It's only what I expected.'

How else could Jan take that but as an admission of his guilt and negligence? Conscious of Stephanie sitting between them, nothing more was said on the subject. Jan doubted that anything more would have been said even if Stephanie hadn't been there.

His forethought meant that she was able to serve up a deliciously cooked meal of steak, button mushrooms, buttered new potatoes and salad. Followed by a chocolate pudding that was Stephanie's particular favourite, and always went down well with adults as well.

She had taken extra pains with the meal, hoping to prove that she was not the feather-brain he imagined her to be. She had always loved cooking, and had been an apt pupil,

27

progressing from the guidance her mother was equipped to give her to more adventurous book recipes, and last year she had attended an advanced cookery class at nightschool. Not quite sure about David's taste she had opted for simplicity and perfection.

'At least you can cook,' he said.

This praise, negative though it was, was gratefully received. Jan's own appreciation did not match up. She was developing a sore, scratchy throat and the steak, though tender enough, was difficult to swallow.

'Do you mind waiting for your coffee until I've put Stephanie to bed? It's later than her normal bedtime.'

'I'm pleased to hear that. I was beginning to wonder.'

She knew she must not let him goad her, so swallowing on that unjust criticism she said stoically: 'She was granted an extension tonight because you are here.' And then—this was more in the nature of an enquiry—'I have a room to prepare for you.'

'If you are asking if I intend to stay, the answer is yes. I know there are adequate rooms. And it is my home, Miss Ashton.'

'Of course.'

'By all means see to Stephanie first, Jan,' he said falling into automatic use of her first name. 'Then, you realise we must talk?'

'Yes, Da—Mr. Spedding,' Jan replied heavily, feeling that she knew just what course

28

that talk would take. It was annoying but natural for her to trip up and almost call him David. Annabel had always referred to him so, and it was the name she thought of him by.

'David will do very nicely.' He didn't add, 'for the short length of time you will be here,' but he might as well have done.

Stephanie went up the stairs docilely enough, but she was too wide awake for Jan's liking. The meal had been too rich an indulgence for a little girl. The chocolate pudding, just before going to bed, had been a mistake. She had been showing off, trying to impress him what a good cook she was. She hoped her pride wasn't going to be taught a sharp lesson in humility. But Stephanie had been so delighted to have her daddy home that Jan hadn't had the heart to give her an earlier nursery supper and pack her off to bed.

'I've got a tummy ache,' Stephanie announced.

'Lay quite still, darling, and it will go off.'

Stephanie didn't want to lay quite still. She wanted to sit up, hug her knees and talk. Then she wanted a story. In sympathy with Stephanie over the loss of her mother, 'No' was a word that Jan hadn't been able to bring herself to use very often. As she succumbed to the 'Just one more story' plea, Jan realised she had a spoilt child on her hands.

When, eventually, she did manage to sneak back downstairs, it was to find that David had

29

washed the dishes and made the coffee. She gratefully accepted her cup, too weary to say, 'You shouldn't have bothered. You should have left it to me.'

'It's no good closing your lashes on me,' he rebuked sternly, as though she was feigning weariness to get out of that proposed, and dreaded, talk.

She jerked awake. Not lacking in courage, she decided to attack in a bold and direct manner. 'You're going to fire me, aren't you?'

There was something insulting in the quantity of lazy amusement in his voice. 'I must. Now that I'm here, there is nothing to keep you. There is not a single reason why you shouldn't leave in the morning.'

She gasped. Her chin lifted in defiance. 'So soon? It will break Stephanie's heart.'

It was silly of her to appeal to his better nature. He hadn't got one!

'Melodramatic nonsense! Hearts don't break that easily.'

How she managed to restrain herself she would never know. It was on the tip of her impetuous tongue to say, 'You speak from experience, of course.' As it was she said angrily: 'You're not being fair.'

'I am being practical,' he corrected emphatically. 'You are not old enough for the responsibilities of the job. It's obvious, even on short acquaintance, that Stephanie would be a handful for a worldlier, more experienced woman.'

A short acquaintance! Incredibly, he was referring to his own daughter! Her determination strengthened.

He continued in that irritatingly smooth fashion of his, 'How can a child like you be expected to cope?'

How dare he call her a child? Was he forgetting that she had carried the den single-handed, while he'd chosen to be absent? How dare he be so cool and mocking and superior? How dare he look at her as though the idea of her being engaged for the job in the first place was an amusing joke!

He seemed to be observing the expressions that chased across her face. His findings caused him to say tautly: 'I am sorry you are taking this as a personal slight. It's not meant that way. The original error was not all yours.'

'You think that when I applied for the job, I should have been turned down as being unsuitable?'

'That is precisely what I think.'

'But I was set on. And I've coped.' She bit her lip and said in weary resignation, 'But that's not the real reason, is it? You're not dismissing me because you think I lack maturity, but because I talked too much earlier on in the Coffee Bean?'

'My dear girl, the one is inseparable from the other. Youth and indiscretion go together. You were merely acting your age, and what could be more natural? So while not exactly blaming you, I am unwilling to keep someone on I see as a danger to something that is personal to me and not a subject for general discussion. I am referring, of course, to my privacy.'

Contemplating the case he put before her with a sinking heart, she made a belated attempt to apologise. 'Privacy is something I respect. I promise never to infringe on yours again.'

Abandoning humour, and that mocking, supercilious drawl she had found so disagreeable, he said with a seriousness that Jan found even more disconcerting, 'I am not prepared to take the risk. You should have counted to ten before opening up to a complete stranger.'

She cautioned herself, *don't* panic. Just tell the truth and everything will be all right. The truth never lets you down.

But she was panicking. Not only that, she was seething with pent-up fury and frustration. His calm and polite pose was unnerving. He was doing it on purpose, of course. His contrasting coolness was cruel provocation. It was a deliberate and well-thought out manoeuvre to goad her into a state of quivering anger. She was so incensed she could hardly keep a limb still.

She swallowed and said with painful effort: 'Is it any good saying that I had a strong suspicion that I knew who you were? It wasn't the indiscretion you took it to be. I thought it was a good way of telling you a few home-truths. I realise now that it was silly of me, but I was hitting back.'

'My compliments on a most touching and inventive effort,' he replied cynically.

'But it's the truth,' Jan claimed, nonplussed.

After all, the truth would not suffice. She wondered at her own gullible expectation that he would even recognise it. What dealings would he have had with truth and honesty and integrity? Such things were outside his comprehension. Hearsay had been proved right. He was devious and heartless and she hated him with a depth of feeling that shocked her gentle soul.

'Tomorrow I want you out,' he said in a low voice that challenged her brave spirit and filled her with trepidation. 'That is my final word.'

'But not mine,' she flung back at him with assumed bravado.

CHAPTER TWO

If she hadn't felt so quivery she would have stayed to argue. She seemed to need her energy to crawl upstairs.

The staircase twisted up to a half-landing with a window on one side and a bedroom leading off. It wasn't very large, but as she sorted out clean sheets which smelt of the sunshine they had been dried in, she thought David would be comfortable here. More's the pity.

Annabel hadn't been able to manage the tortuous narrow stairs, and the front parlour had been converted into a bedroom for her. It had since reverted back to its original use.

Jan continued up the stairs to the main landing which gave access to the remaining two bedrooms. Stephanie's bedroom had a fiercely sloping roof and nursery wallpaper depicting characters from her favourite nursery rhymes. Jan's room was the smallest, but it had the best view. She wondered why nobody had thought to knock out the tiny window and replace it with a larger one to make the best advantage of the beautiful countryside.

Tonight she was in no mood for window-gazing. She abandoned her clothes, dragged on her nightgown and slid into bed. The ceiling began to spin. She had an ominous suspicion that temper alone hadn't been responsible for her shaking limbs. Of all the times to fall ill.

A million or so years later, her bedroom door opened. A voice commanded: 'Wake up, will you!' It was a very irritated sounding, pressing sort of voice. 'I'll be hanged if I'm going to apologise for disturbing you, because it's your own stupidity that makes it necessary. Are you totally irresponsible, or simply lacking in commonsense? Don't you know enough to appreciate that you can't indulge a child to excess without facing the inevitable and unpleasant consequences. Stephanie has been sick.' He'd been ranting on at a great pace. Now there was an extended pause before he asked: 'Are you all right?'

When he saw for himself that she was in no position to answer, he said with quiet acceptance, minimal fuss and monumental patience: 'Forget I said anything.'

She struggled to sit up, but the effort was too much and she didn't object to the hands on her shoulders easing her back down. She didn't object to anything, and even made little murmurs of ecstasy as the cool fingers touched her burning forehead.

She dearly wished she could speak, but the stabbing pains in her chest made it difficult even to breathe. She wanted to ask, no beg, no plead with him not to leave her. Somehow he seemed to understand this without her having to utter a single word, because he said somewhat disjointedly: 'Only for a little while. I promise I'll be back.'

It was the promise she remembered and not the desolate sound of his receding footsteps.

True to his word he came back. 'Steph's okay now. What am I going to do about you?'

Jan was happy to let that be his problem.

After all that had gone before, after being strong and capable and cheerfully coping, it was heaven to shrug off the burden and let someone else be responsible for her.

The cool sponge on her hot cheeks and forehead was the nearest thing to bliss she'd ever experienced, and the voice was so blessedly gentle as the impersonal fingers worked on the buttons of her nightdress.

'Sorry about this, but what choice have I? I can't leave you in this state. If I were a doctor it would be all right. In a way I am, but it's not the right category. The truth is, I'm more used to dealing with rats and mice than people. You think I'm a rat, don't you? Perhaps it would help if I thought of you as a mouse. The trouble is, you don't look like a mouse and you certainly don't act like one. Can't you help me? You could at least push your arm in. Ah! Got it. You'll feel more comfortable now.'

She did. For a little while. Then she began to shiver and burn again, and this nightdress, too, became soaked in perspiration. Whereupon the gentle ministrations, accompanied by the soothing voice, began all over again.

Her throat was unbearably dry. If only she could ask for a drink. She tried to speak, but all she managed was a croak. It didn't matter. He was here again and as before he exactly anticipated her needs. The rim of the cup touched her lips and the cool liquid eased the dryness.

As the fever took hold, her mind started to wander. In moments of consciousness she recognised Doctor Ives. What was he doing here? Was someone sick? Concentration was achieved only with the greatest of difficulty, and the effort to reason proved too much. She gave up the unequal struggle and slid back into the secure and safe world of her childhood. Back into the golden world of sun and buttercups, books and pansy-faced kittens. Every moment of every day crammed to the brim with happiness, except for that one time. She didn't want to think about that time, but instead of marching quickly by, her thoughts stuck there.

'Are we going to Gran's for tea, Mummy?'

'Not today, dear. Gran is very ill.' Too young to appreciate the full implication, she was not too young to soak up the fear and the sadness in her mother's voice as she explained with gentle optimism, 'I must go to Gran's house and stay with her for a little while. Just until she's better.'

'Can't I come with you? Please let me.'

'No, my darling. You're better off here. It wouldn't be any fun for you. And, anyway, what about poor Daddy? You must stay and keep him company.'

At that point a masculine note of persuasion had entered the argument. 'How would I manage the shopping, sweetie-pie, if you weren't on hand to nudge me which brands to buy?'

Daddy was so silly. It wasn't just the shopping, he didn't seem to know anything at all about girls' clothes. He thought that buttons should fasten on the other side, and no matter how firmly he tied her ribbon in her hair, and sometimes it was so tight it seemed to lift her scalp, it always slipped off. If Mummy didn't come home soon, she wouldn't have any hair-ribbons left. Why didn't she come? A tear slid down her cheek.

'Hey, what's this?' A man—Daddy?—asked.

She tried to smile for him and for extra measure she lifted her arms up round his neck, pulled his head down, and gave him a big kiss.

Lucidity returned for a brief moment, long enough for her to realise she had just kissed David Spedding, but not long enough for her to bother about it.

She sensed now that someone was there besides David and she didn't mean Doctor Ives. The hands tending her were more sure of themselves, less awkward and much smaller than David's. She opened her eyes and the anxiety in them faded at the friendly reassurance on the face of the woman looking down at her. 'All right, my lamb?' the woman enquired, and Jan nodded weakly and went back to sleep.

Jan had no notion of time. It could have been seconds, hours, or even days later when David came in. She was sitting up in bed and taking notice—of the fact that while she had been ill he had looked after her beautifully. With only the assistance of a doctor's prescription? Oh no! Please don't let her have dreamt the presence of a woman. She thought she might have. If David had got someone to help out and do the 'lady's maiding' but, surely it would have been a neighbour? Mrs. Weaver next door was the likeliest person to call on. But she was a widow who didn't much like living alone, and she spent most of her time visiting relatives. She'd confided to Jan once that she was the eldest of a large family. Jan thought she had five sisters and three brothers. As she had four children herself, when it came to visiting she had plenty to go to. The woman Jan thought had been looking after her had a face that didn't fit anybody she knew.

'M'm, this is an improvement,' David said.

With the question still unresolved in her mind, she found she couldn't look directly at him. Her glance fixed on his hands. 'Thank you for looking after me,' she said, but to her horror it didn't just come out sounding prim, it sounded stiff and ungracious to the point of being resentful.

'My pleasure.' This cliché did nothing to minimise her embarrassment. After an unforgivably long pause he said: 'I had help.'

Now that she could look at him she saw that he was grinning in huge enjoyment of the joke. She could have hit him.

'I thought someone was here. But who is she? Where is she? Why didn't you call a neighbour in?'

All the tilting-to-laughter lines of his face turned down into a frown. He said with a touch of irritation that conveyed his annoyance, 'I'm not on those sort of terms with the neighbours. When I walk down the street I don't get as much as a 'Good day' so how could I ask for help?'

'Sorry. I'd forgotten.' Forgotten that local opinion had a down on him for his cruel desertion of Annabel and his child. 'I'm also sorry I've been a nuisance to you,' she said in a small voice. 'I've had many worse soakings, with not as much as a sniff to tell of my foolishness.'

She knew he regarded her as an exasperating infant, but he didn't have to make it so obvious. He could have tempered his tone and guarded his expression.

'You must know it wasn't the chill alone. That might have been the final straw, but it wasn't the root cause. I didn't know, until Doctor Ives told me, that you'd looked after Annabel singlehanded. Little wonder it drained you both physically and mentally. Goodness knows how, but somehow you managed to stave off the inevitable reaction until I arrived to take over, and then you gave in.' His expression grew thoughtful without surrendering that cool look of censure. 'I'm frankly puzzled. Why were you such a little idiot? I don't understand why you had to do everything yourself.'

'Doctor Ives said I coped excellently.'

'That's the whole point. Doctor Ives shouldn't have let you. Why didn't you get a qualified nurse for Annabel? Failing that, I'm sure you are on good enough terms with the neighbours to have been able to get someone in to lend a hand. It would have been better than taking the whole load on yourself.'

Jan agreed wholeheartedly. Unfortunately there hadn't been the money to pay for private nursing, and it was typical of Annabel that she wouldn't have a neighbour in, although the offers of assistance had been plentiful. She had always prided herself on showing a bright face, and that was the face she wanted to be remembered by, not the face with the lines of suffering etched so deeply that the cosmetic camouflage no longer sufficed. So, scrupulously endeavouring not to neglect Stephanie, Jan had tackled everything that was asked of her and more besides, and if she were honest with herself it was the one thing she couldn't give to Annabel, a new lease of life, that was the most wearisome burden of all to bear.

Sleep became a luxury, and towards the very end even cat-napping in a chair was denied her, but she never lost sympathy with Annabel's pride. The pride that had given her the courage and seen her through the earlier traumas of being confined to a wheelchair, never wavered, and from the respect she couldn't deny Annabel, an unlikely bond had been forged. The loyalty Jan had given to Annabel then, held good now.

She rounded on David with blazing eyes. 'Didn't you know your wife at all?'

He took an involuntary step towards her and Jan's chin tilted forward to challenge his raised hand. Whatever his first intention, the hand carried on up and swept through his dark hair. Had he really been going to strike her and then had second thoughts?

'My . . . wife,' he said tonelessly.

Did he find it difficult to reconcile Annabel in his thoughts as his wife? Of course he'd never lived with her after going through that sham marriage ceremony. In sickness and in health hadn't meant very much to him, she thought in bitter condemnation.

He said loftily: 'I have no intention of defending my actions. I don't care what you think of me.' And then his tone took on a musing note, it was as if he wasn't talking to her at all but raking through his own painful thoughts. 'Annabel's pride. Ah . . . yes! Even in death that must be protected irrespective of what suffering it causes or to whom.' His eyes flicked back to hers again and although savouring of sarcasm, there was a look in them that didn't so much repel as have her biting on her breath in sympathy for him. 'I owe you an apology, Jan. It was wrong of me to call you a little idiot for going to ridiculous lengths at personal cost to protect Annabel's pride. I should be the last to pass judgement. I, too, have gone to extremes to protect that pride.'

What a strange thing for him to say. What did he mean? What had he done? He'd dipped his hand in his pocket to pay her excessive bills, and Jan didn't doubt that he would have paid for her to have a private nurse if he'd been approached, but that wasn't the same as being with her. She had been wrong in accusing him of not knowing Annabel. He knew about her pride.

'I would also like to apologise. I was wrong in thinking you didn't know Annabel.'

'No, you were right. I thought I knew Annabel once. But when it came down to it, I didn't know her at all.'

'You knew about her pride. At the end, that was all she had left. I cared for her by myself, because she was too proud to let anybody else see her.'

David stopped frowning into the distance and roused himself to say: 'I ought to say a few words about Linda, to prepare you. Then she won't come as so much of a shock.'

Intrigued, Jan said: 'Presumably Linda is the lady who has been looking after me.'

'Yes. At times she entertains some weird notions. And she is too outspoken, as you are about to find out,' he said as the door opened

43

and in walked a youthful-looking, but not young, smiling woman.

'Hello, Jan. Good to see you sitting up and taking notice. I'm Linda Brookes. Hugh, my husband, and David are work colleagues. But you'll know all about that and just what I am to David. How clever of him to find you.'

Jan saw what David meant about Linda having weird notions. She corrected: 'He didn't find me. I was foisted on him, much to his regret.'

'That's very coy of you, Jan, and I don't believe a word of it.'

Jan sighed. 'Anyway, thank you for looking after me.'

'Not too much gratitude, please, or I shall feel guilty. Hugh made me come. He said it was my duty to rally round, but it's been my pleasure. You've been a delight to look after. But I dread to think how my dear husband is getting along. He's a genius in the lab and takes things in his stride that turns my hair white at the thought, but in its own mundane way the kitchen can be a deathtrap to a man whose head is filled with—'

The look David sent Linda effectively shushed her. Yet, somehow, at the same time he managed to combine the deference her age, or possibly social standing, demanded. Not that Linda Brookes was the type to be intimidated by the likes of David.

As she returned his look, her head tilted

44

elegantly on her long, swan neck, accentuated to look more swanlike by the severely short haircut which only someone with the advantage of ultra feminine features could take. At twenty she must have been breathtaking, at fifty or thereabouts, she could still raise a gasp of envy in Jan's throat. Not, strictly speaking, because of her pretty features, but for the affectionate way she admonished David.

'I get enough of Hugh going on, without you starting. I've no intention of giving anything away that Jan shouldn't know. Anyway, it might be the most fascinating thing on earth to you, but from a feminine slant of things it's frankly boring. So there! And if that hasn't put you in your place, let me tell you that neither Jan nor I are the type to gossip indiscriminately. Right, Jan?'

Because he was listening, Jan would have blushed at that anyway and David didn't need to send her a prolonged and doubting look.

Her hair gently slapped her cheeks as her chin went from side to side. 'Speak for yourself. My track record isn't so hot.'

The gleam of gentle humour in Linda's eyes was not replaced by rue as she obviously thought it was something or nothing. Her apology was blatant lip-service. 'Sorry if I've edged you on to delicate ground, Jan.'

She hasn't a clue, thought Jan. She thinks I'm on safe ground with David.

'Is he in a mood? Shall I tactfully make myself scarce and then you can distract him out of it? In any case, I'd better pop down and see what Stephanie is doing. That little one is a boxful of tricks. I left her having breakfast, which reminds me. Fancy some yourself? A lightly coddled egg on toast?'

'A cup of tea would go down better,' Jan admitted.

'I'll do the egg on toast and if you really can't face it, I won't complain if you don't eat it.'

When she'd gone, David said: 'You must start eating again. Try for Linda's sake.'

'I will. She's nice.'

'I think so, and have thought so for longer than I can remember. Her husband, Hugh, is my boss. They've only been married just over a year. Before that Hugh was married to his work, he's one of our most distinguished research chemists, and I'm honoured to be on his team. Linda was a highly paid "ideas woman" for a cosmetic firm, or house as she calls it. She says she was always too busy supplying the bait for other women's traps to bother about snaring her own, but when she met Hugh she had all the tricks of her trade at her fingertips and the poor man didn't stand a chance.'

Jan laughed. 'Linda hinted at some tie between you and her. Are you related?'

'She's my godmother. A position which, she

feels, gives her certain privileges. She can be very stubborn when she gets a bee in her bonnet about something.'

'Judging by your expression, she's buzzing something up for you at the moment.'

'I really ought to spare your blushes by not telling you. Remember, you did ask. She's so happily married herself that she thinks everybody else should follow suit. Me in particular.'

She wondered if David's romantically minded godmother had her matchmaking eye fixed on anybody special. What did David mean about sparing her blushes? Oh no! Linda couldn't think there was anything like that going on between her and David! It was too preposterous.

'Are your pillows comfy?' David asked innocently.

'Not very.'

She wasn't feeling comfortable at all, but it wasn't the fault of her flattened pillows.

She twisted sideways, as if to plump them up, not realising that David was bending forward with that same intention in mind. The collision was unavoidable.

'Sorry,' David said, automatically grasping her by the shoulders to steady her.

It was like being hit by a thunderbolt. She willed her body to remain detached as her heart leapt at the feel of his fingers through the demure cover-up of her bedjacket. His

47

hands let go so quickly that she thought he must know of her heart's shame. Never before had she had to bolster her resistance against any man's advances, and David's innocent steadying touch couldn't be called that. It was heinous of her to respond with such vital insistence. Yet was the blame wholly hers? Hadn't David started it by telling her that Linda hoped to see him happily married? Sold on marriage herself after years of indifference, she wanted her godson to meet and fall in love with a nice girl and know the bliss of a happy union, something he hadn't experienced in his marriage to Annabel. And that's where Linda's kindly thoughts went sour. It was too soon after Annabel's death for David's possible interest in another girl to be in anything but the most deplorable taste. She could believe the worst of David, but it was difficult to endow Linda with the same low standards. Linda had struck her as being a person of faultless propriety and unimpeachable taste.

'Permit me,' David said, and deftly plumped up and rearranged her pillows, this time making sure not to touch her. He then requested formally: 'When you've had breakfast, is it all right if I bring Stephanie up to see you? I promise I won't let her stay long enough to tire you.'

'Of course. I'm longing to see her. She must think I've deserted her.' Oh dear, surely she could have worded it a bit more tactfully than that.

A look of pain pierced David's eyes so briefly that Jan wondered if she'd imagined it. Certainly now his eyes expressed only coldness as he said: 'As I deserted her and Annabel?' He made it sound like a question, as if it were not an established and unarguable fact. 'What was it about Annabel that inspired such loyalty, I wonder?'

There was no ready reply on Jan's lips and a confusion of thoughts in her head.

'Please excuse me,' he said. 'I'll be back presently with Stephanie.' His smile, though slight, had a gentleness about it that seemed to encompass Jan's numb heart.

The click of the door as it closed behind him activated her thoughts. Whose loyalty had he been referring to? Hers? Of course hers! He hadn't been referring to his own. He'd shown none. And yet she found herself recalling David's words about her going to ridiculous lengths at personal cost to protect Annabel's pride. What else had he said? 'I, too, have gone to extremes to protect that pride.' The words became an abrasive on Jan's memory. She put them from her, but they scratched their way to the surface again, as if she was missing a significance that was vital to her understanding of him. But what was there to understand? He'd married a beautiful and vivacious young woman, who just happened to be pregnant with his child, but on their way to the wedding reception the car they were travelling in met with an accident. The driver of the car, Stephen Grant, a family friend, died instantly, and Annabel suffered terrible injuries which confined her to a wheelchair for the rest of her life. A crippled wife was not in his reckoning—so exit David. She was a fool to sift his words in search of something, she knew not what, that might put a different light on the situation. There was only one possible explanation. David was a rat.

One favoured with above average looks, who had been given an extra helping of charm to make up for not having a heart.

But how could she say that he didn't have a heart after the thoughtful way he had taken care of her? Indisputably he had charm to spare, no grounds for argument there. It crept into his eyes and settled on the wayward lift of his smile. And although it was a commodity he had in abundance, he was cunning enough to use it sparingly, so that when he did it knocked her legs from under her.

She could hate him, but she couldn't help herself from falling under the spell of his fatal fascination. That was it! He had cast a spell over her. Could she resist it? It was a question she must answer truthfully and if the answer was no then she'd do herself a favour by getting out of his life as fast as she could.

But if she did, what about Stephanie, the

little girl so recently bereaved of her mother? Because of his initial desertion, her father was a stranger. Children don't like changes, they are more at home with that which is familiar. They like to feel safe. Jan was the obvious link between her old life and the new one which faced her. Stephanie had to be the one to sever that link, not Jan. She had to do it by herself and in her own good time, and that wouldn't be until she felt a lot more secure than she did now.

Linda came in with the breakfast tray. The egg was superbly cooked, the toast was temptingly trimmed of its hard crust, but Jan's valiant best amounted to only a mouthful.

'I'm sorry, Linda.'

'That's all right. Perhaps you're not an eggy person. Can I get you something else?'

'No, really. I'm just not hungry.'

'Oh well, you'll come to your corn when you are. You look heaps better this morning. Almost perky enough for me to think about going home to my Hugh. I've missed him,' she said reflectively. 'Does that sound sloppy?'

'Of course not. It sounds rather nice. People in love should want to be together.'

'That's true. When you get to my age the span of life starts ebbing faster. I begrudge all the years I've spent without my beloved Hugh. And yet it makes me value the time we have now more than if we had a lifetime ahead of us to fritter away. I'm so happy myself, that I want everyone else to be happy. Because he's always had a special place in my heart, I want David to be happy. He's had more pain and misery in his life than most his age, and precious little happiness these last few years. I don't know if David is for you or you are for him, but if you are, Jan . . . Oh it is difficult, when I can't say what I think should be said. Let me put it another way. Let your inherent good sense guide and influence you. Don't be fooled into thinking that something is true because enough people say it is. Always remember that silence isn't necessarily an admission of guilt.'

Jan said wistfully: 'I wish someone loved me as much as you love your godson.'

Hope polished the older woman's eyes. 'It's there, Jan, I know it. It's up to you to let it happen.' But her beseeching smile turned wry when she saw the indulgent but disbelieving look Jan was giving her.

Jan was not unaware of this. She knew about her giveaway face. Had she thought about it in time she would have guarded her expression. On reflection it was better this way. Better for Linda to know the score and turn her matchmaking eye on some other, less idealistic girl.

Linda wasn't a stranger to wise words, but where David was concerned she had a blind spot.

Linda lifted the breakfast tray off the bed,

resting it on one hip. 'Do you feel up to Stephanie now?'

The way the question was put was very revealing. Hadn't the combined efforts of David and Linda proved adequate to the task of dissuading Stephanie from getting up to monkey tricks? Jan's thoughts dwelt affectionately on the little girl with the sweet pixie face framed in feather curls that had taken neither of her parents' dark colouring, but was the soft gold of the morning sun. To look deep into her sparkling eyes was to know that her excitable nature would all too frequently entice her into mischief.

The young lady of her thoughts came bouncing into the room, an unlikely combination of indignation and delight stamped on her features. 'How could you get poorly, Jan? Tatty Bear didn't like it. He's glad you're better.'

Annabel had once picked Teddy up and said, 'He's in such a sorry state he should be called Tatty Bear and not Teddy Bear,' and the name had stuck.

'You can tell Tatty Bear from me that I wasn't too keen myself. I'm glad to be better, too. To make it up to him, just as soon as I'm up and about, we'll have to think up some special treat.'

'Ooh, yes!' Stephanie's eyes shone like gemstones.

Annabel's eyes had been blue, David's were

brown. Somehow they had produced a green-eyed child. Not the vivid grass green of an emerald, but the softer, more subtle green of a peridot. Her pretty child's features gave a hint of the beauty she would one day be, but it was the unusual colour of her eyes that would give her beauty its rare and exceptional quality. At four, her capacity to charm and beguile was frightening. Jan hoped that somewhere in her developing personality there was enough commonsense and wisdom for her to—a strange thought—but to triumph over her exceptional looks and remain sweet and unspoilt.

Clapping her hands in ecstatic expectation, Stephanie wanted to know what treat Tatty Bear would like best.

She should have been prepared for this one. She had spoken on impulse without giving the matter due thought. 'Let me see . . . a trip to the zoo to see his cousins, maybe? A ride on a train, do you think? Or a picnic in Willowby Woods. Tatty Bear loves picnics.'

David, who had come in with Stephanie, said promptly and much to Jan's grudging respect and greater surprise: 'He told me in confidence that he'd like a tidy house. Tatty Bear says he's fed up with a place that's littered with toys that *someone* has brought out and not put back.'

Jan liked the understanding that had developed between David and his small

54

daughter. Stephanie was deplorably untidy and must be taught to respect her toys and return them to their proper place when she'd tired of playing with them. Annabel's excessive indulgence had sabotaged Jan's attempts at training Stephanie to be tidy. Communicating with the child through the toy bear to get her to do something she didn't want to do wasn't new to Jan. She had often used the ploy, 'Tatty Bear says he's sleepy and it's time he was tucked up in bed,' but she had thought David would adopt a superior male attitude and consider that sort of approach to be too soft.

'Tatty Bear says it is a tidy house,' Stephanie said, her mutiny softened by a smile. 'He's just told me.'

'In that case, I think we'd better take a trip to the optician's.'

Before Jan could open her mouth to say that Stephanie wouldn't know the meaning of the word optician, David had gone on to explain: 'That's a sort of shop where you go to have your eyes tested when you need glasses. If Tatty Bear sees a tidy house, then obviously he needs glasses.'

'Black ones like Mrs. Grant wears?' Stephanie asked, looking intrigued. She referred to the tinted lenses worn by Willowbridge's first lady.

Both Jan and Linda found it necessary to subdue giggles, but a shadow crossed David's features and a bleak and bedevilled look came

55

to his eyes.

It must be the after-effects of her illness because usually she was brighter than this. Of course Stephanie's reference to Mrs. Grant would stir unpleasant memories. Louisa Grant's son, Stephen, had died in the car crash that had injured Annabel.

For the first time Jan felt a twinge of sympathy for him. He wasn't totally uncaring. His handling of Stephanie proved that he was capable of giving love; having the wit to communicate through Tatty Bear had uncovered a streak of sensitivity that was rare in men. Deserting a wife wasn't punishable by law, but it came to Jan that it was a misdeed that would likely haunt him for the rest of his life.

'When can I get up?' Jan asked.

'As soon as you feel able to,' David replied. 'But not to work. I'm standing no nonsense. Until you've got your full strength back, I insist that you put your feet up and do nothing.'

'When I've got my strength back, I'll retaliate. The days of the dictator boss have gone.'

She was laughing; he wasn't.

'When you're strong enough to retaliate, you won't be here.'

'What do you mean, I won't be here?'

The look in his eye told her he wasn't hoodwinked by her pretend non-comprehension. His tone was dry with

56

exasperation. 'The moment you're fit enough to travel, I'm sending you back home. I gave you your marching orders before you became ill. Had you forgotten?'

'No,' she replied with dignity and truth, plus a controlled spurt of anger. 'I hadn't forgotten. I was hoping you had though.' She didn't add 'for Stephanie's sake,' but her eyes glanced to where the child was playing with childlike lack of concern. She didn't look up from the all-important task of making a neckerchief for Tatty Bear out of her handkerchief. Children can be very cruel at times. She consoled herself with the thought that Stephanie hadn't properly understood that she was being sent home. It couldn't be because she didn't care.

Somebody cared. Linda cared.

'I wouldn't be too hasty if I were you, David. Think twice before you decide that you can cope on your own.'

'I've no intention of coping on my own.'

'You weren't counting on me?'

'No. I'm on the look-out for a woman. Someone mature and sensible.'

'That's all right then. And now I'm going to phone Hugh to tell him that I'm on my way home.'

'Now?'

'Dear boy, you look surprised.'

'I am. I didn't think you'd be rushing off in such a hurry. I thought you might stay long enough to tide me over . . .' He frowned. 'Can

57

we talk this over in private?'

'Certainly. But you won't change my mind.'

The private conversation was not related to Jan, but not long after it took place, Linda draped her car coat over her suitcase, and sought Jan out to say goodbye.

'You are doing it on purpose, aren't you, Linda?'

'What do you mean? I told you that now you'd perked up I was going home.'

'You said you were thinking about it, which implied soon, tomorrow or the next day. It wasn't a decision of desperate urgency. You're shooting off at a moment's notice because you think if David is left to cope while I'm still wobbly on my feet, it will give him a taste of what looking after Stephanie is all about, and that he might change his mind and let me stay.'

'I couldn't have put it better myself,' Linda admitted on a little laugh.

'Thank you, anyway, for the kind thought.'

'Kind, but not very bright? You're right, of course. If David has made up his mind to send you home, neither my tongue nor my absence will make him change it. You'd think I'd learn, wouldn't you? I haven't been able to influence him about the other matter, and goodness knows I've tried. Oh, he does infuriate me!' She stopped, but only to draw breath and not to chain her tongue. 'With a name like his, you'd think he'd stone to death the Goliath of Local Opinion that's damning him.'

58

It always came back to that.

'Perhaps he hasn't the right stone,' Jan said carefully, knowing it would seem that she was siding with local opinion. As indeed she was. She had condemned him along with everyone else.

Linda gave an impassioned gasp. 'But he has!'

'If it's a misconception, if that's what you're hinting at, then why doesn't he throw that stone and shatter it?'

'Because stones have a habit of reverberating. This one definitely would. The most innocent party would get hurt.'

What could Linda mean? The most innocent party was Stephanie. If, somehow, David had the means to justify his actions, how could that harm his daughter? Surely it would be to her benefit to have a father who was accepted by the local community?

'I've said more than I should already. Please don't ask me to explain,' Linda beseeched. 'Goodbye, love. Don't overdo things at first.'

'I won't. Goodbye, Linda. Safe journey. And thank you for coming to look after me. I'm very grateful.'

'Bless you for being so sweet. I'll give you a tinkle to let you know I've arrived safe. 'Bye.'

*   *   *

Stephanie was in bed. The effort of getting up

had taken its toll more than Jan was prepared to admit, and she didn't intend to be long behind her. She replaced the telephone receiver after taking Linda's promised call, a thoughtful expression on her face. Not because of something Linda had just said, that conversation had been the usual light inconsequential telephone talk, but because her mind had reverted to Linda's earlier words when she had strongly hinted that David wasn't the villain people made out. She was too tired to puzzle it out now. She would think about it tomorrow.

*   *   *

She thought about it tomorrow and the next day and the day after that, at the supper table, she was still thinking about it.

'Is your indifference passing unfavourable judgement on what is definitely one of my better culinary efforts?'

'No.' She picked up her knife and fork and resumed eating. 'It's delicious. I feel a terrible fraud letting you do everything. Can I take over again tomorrow, please? I'm quite well now.'

These last three days had given her a glimpse of the David whom Linda knew and loved. Back to the puzzle. It would have been better if Linda hadn't said anything, rather than pique her curiosity in this frustrating way.

If there was something that David could say ... She wasn't aware of it but her chin gave an involuntary little shake. No. She must keep quiet. She mustn't interfere. But ...

The 'but' was stronger insistence than she could bear. 'David?'

'Yes?'

His voice was too sharp for comfort. She didn't know that he had been quietly surveying the conflict of emotions disturbing the serenity of her features.

'Nothing,' she said backing down. 'It's none of my business.'

'Good. Let's keep it that way.'

The temperament of Grandmother Ashton in her rose to the surface at the taunt in his voice. The above-the-table lamp glanced across her hair as her chin tilted, bringing the red highlights into play. The tranquil green left her eyes and the storm-warning brown bounced with points of angry light.

'It's not good enough. Don't you see, you are damning yourself by your own silence. If you don't talk you won't be able to live here in peace and comfort, and no matter where you move it will be the same, because the gossip and the whispering behind your back will follow you. You've got to speak up to shut them up.'

'How did you find out?' he said in such an ominously quiet voice that all the fire in her turned to ice. Except that ice doesn't feel, and even in fear of him she was still quivering with emotion. 'What a nice person you are,' he mocked, the tone of his voice an insult. 'An indiscriminate gossip, and a snoop! You must have rifled the desk and pried into papers that are no concern of yours.'

In her entire twenty years, Jan had never knowingly pried into affairs that were none of her business. She had only encountered the Sheraton desk to dust it and slide the unpaid bills waiting for David's attention into a small drawer that was separate from the main part of the cylinder-top desk. The key that operated the roll-back front sat permanently in its lock, but Jan had never been tempted to turn it. How could David make such an accusation?

'No!' she said in vehement denial.

His eyes narrowed. His anger matched her own. 'Don't add lies to your other transgressions. How else could you know?'

She opened her mouth to speak, then stopped. After all she couldn't defend herself. She couldn't say that she didn't really know anything, but she'd gleaned from the little Linda had told her that it wasn't all as it seemed. She couldn't implicate Linda.

She blinked her eyelids to seal in the tears that were two parts vexation and one part of something that was beyond analysis.

'You've got to speak up,' she said through wretchedly stiff lips. 'For Stephanie's sake.'

'For . . .?' He threw back his head and—

damn him—he laughed! Laughed! 'That was a near thing. Thinking you knew, I could well have let something slip. But you *don't* know.'

'No, I *don't* know,' she shouted back at him.

He put his finger under her chin, and it stayed there until she obeyed its command and looked into his eyes. 'But you are a proper Jan Pry. You're going to ferret and probe until you find out, aren't you, my inquisitive little friend?'

'Not out of morbid curiosity. I only want what is best for Stephanie.'

'Will you believe that so do I? You mean well, but you could unwittingly harm Stephanie. I can't let you. You've got to go, Jan. I daren't risk the consequences of your staying.'

'I won't go,' she said stupidly, recklessly.

'Don't be silly. If I say you're going, you'll go.'

'Not of my own free will. Not while Stephanie needs me. You'll have to evict me by force.'

'That sort of talk won't get you anywhere with me. I don't give in to emotional blackmail and tantrums are best left to children who don't know any better.' His fingers once again reached out to secure her chin. 'How old did you say you were?'

When he'd first asked her that she'd added a few years on to impress him she was mature enough for the task of looking after Stephanie.

She'd forgotten just how many. 'Twenty-four,' she said not very convincingly.

His face came closer. 'Old enough,' he said. His eyes flicked away from hers and feasted themselves on the slender but gently curved womanliness of her body. Slowly, slumbrously almost, his gloating, mocking, wicked gaze returned to her face. His eyes were dark brown seduction, so near that she had no leeway to shore up her collapsing defences.

'Little Jan. You say you are a woman, but you have the guileless look of a child. And a temper that is childlike. Temper is but a passionate outburst. The child stamps her foot; the woman has better uses for her passions. Let us find out if you are the woman you claim to be.'

Even as her heart lurched at the look in his eye, it didn't occur to her to resist the arms closing round her. Her neck curved back in a gesture of abandon as her body complied in melting obedience to his will.

His kiss was the pure flame. The fierce brutal heat, the flicker of tenderness in its molten core. It carried her along with its irresistible force, and it lit something in her heart that would never die.

He whispered huskily: 'It has been demonstrably proved that you are a woman.' He stroked her cheek. 'Warm, desirable. You could be a lot of fun.'

Fun! Her breath caught between surprise

and outrage. When she looked at him she saw that his head was back and he was laughing.

'Has it got through to you now, my fanciable little peach, that I could chase you out faster than if you had a whirlwind at your heels.'

It wasn't the whirlwind at her heels that bothered her, but the fire in her breast. Her head tilted in magnificent defiance, and he must never know at what cost.

'That was a vile trick to play. You are detestable, despicable and utterly contemptible. A sadist without morals or human caring. I was right about you first time. You're a monster, cruel, heartless . . .' And on it went. She ran out of breath and words simultaneously, and then her eyes more than made up for the incapacity of her tongue.

She felt degraded and humiliated. No matter what tender act he put on in the future, she would never trust him again.

'I'm going to my room now. You can go to the devil.'

'That will probably be my fate.'

The laughter quietened in his eyes. Was this another bit of diabolical trickery, a continuation of the drive-Jan-out campaign, or did he really feel as bemused as he looked? He seemed to have forgotten the name of the game, as if, for a brief moment, control of the situation had slipped out of his masterful grip.

'Sleep well,' he said quite kindly. 'You're perfectly safe.'

'I never thought otherwise,' she tossed back at him haughtily. 'While I'm under your roof, I'm under your protection.'

The gleam was back in evidence. 'In that case, I can only hope your faith in me is justified,' he taunted darkly.

CHAPTER THREE

While she was ill, a temporary truce had been called. Now that she was better, it was war again. He went back to being Awesome Mouth, an implacable stranger who wouldn't listen to her appeal to be allowed to stay for Stephanie's sake, and took every opportunity to treat her like a child. If, sometimes, the mask slipped and he looked at her as though she were a woman, he soon got it back in place again. Her own awareness of him as a man was dealt with just as efficiently.

She had always prided herself on being a resolute person of firm character with a set pattern of beliefs to subscribe to. There was an inseparable link between loving and liking. She couldn't like someone as domineering and as unreasonable as David. She couldn't love someone she didn't like. So where was the problem?

She told herself she was infatuated with the novelty of him. She had never met a man like him before, and she'd never meet the likes of him again, she thought wistfully. She was at it again, cluttering up the issue with her petty feelings, when it was Stephanie who mattered.

'You're not going to let me stay, are you?'

'No.'

'When I've gone, who's going to look after Stephanie?'

'I am.'

'Don't you have a job to follow?'

'I do. I also have a considerable amount of leave due to me. I'm taking it now. When the time comes for me to resume work, I should have got Stephanie sorted out, and I shall leave her in the care of a sensible, mature woman. Right now, she needs a man's hand. You've ruined her.'

No other accusation could have locked her tongue so effectively. It wasn't fair. She hadn't ruined Stephanie. It was Annabel's spoiling that had made Stephanie the unmanageable child she was. But who could blame Annabel for doting on the little girl and cramming a lifetime of spoiling into four years?

She glared at him, as if she could compel him to her way of thinking by force of will.

He laughed. 'I'll allow no female to be my master. My mistress, perhaps.'

'I'm not applying for that job.'

'You'd get short shrift if you were. Take my advice. Go home to your mother, little girl, and do some growing up.'

He backed his advice with a rail ticket. She took Stephanie to play-school one morning, and knew she couldn't be there to fetch her home. She would be—if David didn't change his mind, and he didn't, and so she was—on a train glancing the miles away.

As she neared home, familiar landmarks came into view. One particular landmark which she always looked out for was a huge hoarding advertising a popular brand of paint. Whenever she saw it, she knew she was home. She saw it now, but without exultation. The warm surge of pleasure she would have felt a few weeks ago was completely lacking.

Mr. Hymes, the friendly ticket collector, was the first of many to recognise her and greet her warmly. 'Hello, Jan. Good to see you again.' As she replied she hoped the moistness in her eyes would be put down to home-coming nostalgia. It would be a joy to see her parents. She hadn't phoned to tell them she was coming, because up to the last minute she had hoped that David would change his mind. Anyway, you don't have to be formal with parents. What a surprise they would get.

The surprise was on her. The first clue was the quietness of the house as she let herself in. Her mother always worked with the radio on. She had even been known to take her small transistor into the garden with her to help along her unfavourite task of weeding. Thinking her mother had stepped out to the shops, Jan put the kettle on and went to raid the fridge. No milk. Odd.

Perhaps her mother had realised she was out of milk and had gone to get some. But this thought didn't seem to have a lot of weight to it. In contrast the feeling she had was heavy enough to merit investigation. Upstairs, a count of suitcases told her the worst. One was missing. The medium sized one used for weekending and visits of up to a week's duration.

She went to bed with only the creakings of the old house for company.

Next day was no better. Without a mother in it, the house she had known since childhood wasn't a home. Home was a Yorkshire village, two hundred miles away. Was Stephanie missing her? Had she kicked up a fuss when Jan hadn't been there to meet her yesterday tea-time?

She tried not to think about Stephanie and considered her own plight. She ought to think about getting a job. Because of David's generosity, he'd paid her up to date and added a most handsome bonus because he said her devoted care of Annabel had been over and above the line of duty, it wasn't what you might call a vital issue.

Thoughts of Annabel had resurrected her

69

ghost in her mind. Not a spooky ghost, but a ghost with a bright, devil-may-care, admonishing smile. 'Shame on you,' it chided. Annabel wouldn't have moped. She would have taken a long, self-indulgent look at the situation and said with a defiant and spirited lift of her chin, 'But this isn't helping *me*.' Proud and self-willed, impetuous and fearless to the point of recklessness, she had maintained an envious way of looking at things. Of her own predicament she had said, 'Yesterday wasn't too good. Today will be better.'

David might have walked out on her, but he hadn't found anybody with enough sparkle to replace her.

It was as if Annabel had put a finger to her chin and made her look at the situation squarely. It was all a bit mixed up in her mind, but her thoughts seemed to be following a direction that was not of her pointing, and certainly not to her liking. How could David find comfort or excitement or anything with her, after Annabel?

She brushed the tears away with the back of her hand, rather as a child might have done. The smile that nobody was there to see was a bit wobbly as she turned her attention to practical things. Her mother kept a well-stocked freezer, but if she wanted fresh milk, cheese, eggs and fruit, she would have to make a trip to the supermarket.

Walking down the wide aisles, between the

regimented shelves to the blare of canned music, Jan compared it unfavourably with excursions to Alice Spink's general store where the potatoes were scooped up from a sack, and the yellow country butter was cut from a huge slab. And you weren't fed entertainment from a speaker, you supplied your own. The shop was the focal point of gossip and gossip was the chief source of entertainment. She remembered how she had been taken in by the apparently slower pace, and had even wondered if the transition from a bustling town to this sleepy village atmosphere would be too great. Until it had dawned on her that it was a fallacy and there was more below-the-surface activity than first met the eye. In the early days she had found the ways of the country people strange, touching, artful and sometimes baffling. They would argue like fury amongst themselves, but they were fiercely loyal to their own and Jan had taken it as a compliment when they opened their ranks to her. All she'd had to do then was battle with the mysteries of the local dialect, and once that was mastered she was home and dry. And not averse to picking up the latest bit of gossip with her order!

'Jan! Jan Ashton,' the voice repeated her name insistently. 'I heard you'd returned to civilisation.'

'Hello, Sylvia,' Jan greeted the tall, brown-haired girl coming towards her. She had

71

rounded features, a snub nose, a mouth of generous proportions, and a figure to match. Jan thought it a great pity that her nature wasn't as pretty as she was, and immediately felt guilty for her lack of charity.

'I see the rustic scene hasn't killed you off. Of course, nobody actually dies of boredom. I bet you're glad to be back.'

Jan fought off her attack of nostalgia for Willowbridge and said: 'It's always nice to be home.'

Nothing had altered between them. Although Sylvia's smile beamed on her, it had neither the warmth nor the naturalness of the sun. It was artificial and met no easy response in Jan. And it wasn't just the forced nature of her smile, Jan found it difficult not to recall that it was Sylvia who had told her about Martin's interest in another girl.

'Have you much more to get?' Sylvia asked, inspecting the box of eggs and the pack of cheese in Jan's wire basket.

'Just some apples and milk,' Jan replied.

'I won't be long either. Wait for me beyond the checkout and I'll treat you to a coffee and a Danish.'

She couldn't throw Sylvia's friendly overture back in her face, and besides which she was wondering if she'd misjudged her about the other. Sylvia was so sweetly eager to prolong the meeting that it hardly seemed possible that she had informed her about Martin and Tara out of malice. Or if she had, perhaps she'd had second thoughts and was sorry and dearly wanted to make amends.

'All right,' Jan said, smiling. 'Only I'm flush so the treat's on me.'

'Had a premium bond up or something?'

'No. I've just been paid up.'

'Oh? It's not a holiday break then? Have you had the push?'

Jan wished she hadn't been quite so forthcoming. Sylvia was hardly the best confidante in the world. 'Not really. My employer has quite recently died and my work commitment came to a natural end.'

'Oh!' Sylvia was momentarily nonplussed, although doubtless she would think of some searching questions to ask later.

Over coffee and Danish pastries in the chrome-plated elegance of the adjacent coffee bar (not a patch of the aromatic cosiness of the Coffee Bean at Willowbridge) Sylvia said thoughtfully: 'You look peaky. Have you been pining for Martin?'

Martin had long since been relegated in her mind as a dear and valued friend. They'd lived within a stone's throw of each other and his mother had been 'Aunt' Dora to her, as hers had been 'Aunt' Muriel to him. If Tara hadn't come along, and she hadn't subsequently met David, perhaps they might have drifted into marriage without ever knowing there was a deeper love than the fondness they felt for

73

each other, a love as tender as an early summer breeze, as scorching as a rim of fire.

With the genuine affection she would always feel for Martin, Jan fastened eagerly on to his name. 'How is Martin?'

'He'll be better now that you're back, I shouldn't wonder.'

'Has he been ill?'

Sylvia's round brown eyes went rounder with glee. She had always relished telling a tale. 'You don't know!' she squealed. 'Of course, it's all happened quite recently, but I thought Martin would have written to tell you, or better still, telephoned.'

'About what?'

Sylvia sat back, taking a ghoulish delight in keeping Jan in suspense. 'About his break-up with Tara. Everybody but them knew it couldn't last. I suppose really their temperaments are too much alike. Tara couldn't manage him as beautiful as you did, Jan. She made it plain from the beginning that she wasn't going to follow your lead and pamper him out of his moods. I'm not saying that you were weak to let Martin walk all over you the way he did. I accept that it's some people's nature to do anything for a quiet life, and very nice too if you can square it with yourself to be like that. I wish I could. The world would be a more tranquil place to live in if there were more people like you.'

No, Sylvia hadn't changed. She still

74

possessed the knack of getting under the skin. But Jan felt a niggle of sympathy for her. A reasonably clear picture was emerging. Sylvia had always chased Martin. Martin would be feeling low, and perhaps Sylvia had made a bid for him, but he was too wise to be susceptible to flattery and too wary to be caught on the rebound.

All the same, Jan couldn't resist having a little scratch back. 'Some people think tranquillity is a euphemism for dullness.'

She thought it odd how you could be different things to different people. For example, tranquillity was something David would not associate with her.

'You're not dull. Such a thought never entered my mind.' She looked at her watch and said disbelievingly: 'If little Sylvia doesn't get her skates on she's going to be late again. I've already been ticked off twice this week for being late back from lunch. Work is such a bind. I've still a million things to tell you, and I want to know everything that's happened to you while you've been away. I can't promise for definite, but I might see my way to popping round to your house this evening, if that's all right?'

'I'm not sure. I might be going out,' Jan replied, as offputting as she dare.

'That won't matter. If I come and you're out that will be my hard luck. The walk will do me good.'

75

*　　*　　*

That evening, Jan waited until she was sure Martin would be home from work and then she lifted the telephone and dialled his number.

'Hello, Martin,' she said recognising his voice immediately. 'It's me, Jan.'

'How marvellous! Where are you phoning from, you gorgeous psychic creature? You must have known I needed cheering up.'

'I'm at home.'

'Better and better. When can I see you? Now? If you haven't eaten, perhaps we could grab a bite to eat somewhere. Please say yes, Jan, for old times' sake.'

She didn't want to start anything up again with Martin, but because of the way he'd worded the invitation it would seem churlish of her to refuse. 'Yes, then.'

'Great. Where would you like to go?'

Not sure what he had in mind, a proper meal or a bar snack, she replied: 'I'm not fussy.'

'Neither am I, so long as the steak is good.'

'How about the Horse and Hounds?' She named a venue that had never been one of their special places, safe in the knowledge that he wouldn't think she was retreading memories in the hope of reawakening the romantic interest between them. She had

76

slipped up.

'Anywhere but there, Jan.' His voice sounded pained. 'It was Tara's favourite place.'

'Sorry. I didn't mean to be tactless.'

'That's all right. I realise you couldn't have known.'

'You haven't got over her yet?'

'You've got to be joking. She turned out to be a right bitch. You've no idea how she treated me,' he said in a hurt little voice.

Her inside gave a big sigh of despair. She knew from past experience that Martin in a sorry-for-himself mood was not the happiest of fortunes.

That unlikely beginning preceded an evening that turned up more than one surprising twist. She had thought there might be some constraint or awkwardness between them, but no, they picked up from where they had left off. Which was in itself a thought to ponder over. They had never been lovers, only the warmest of friends. She had been the naïve one to think the little-girl affection she felt was a sufficiently strong feeling to take them into the intimacy of marriage.

Martin had a cultured appearance that did justice to his well-cut lounge suit, and yet had he been wearing casual sweater and jeans, Jan knew he would have looked just as immaculate. He was incredibly good looking. Perhaps his features were too refined for a man, and his light brown hair was too fine and silky and could have done with more bounce. But it was his boyish face that accounted for a high percentage of his charm.

He awarded Jan a devastatingly ponderous look as he declared: 'You have lost a little weight and done a lot of growing up.'

'I should hope so,' she said, deliberately ignoring the slight twinge of regret in his voice. 'Not about the weight, about the other. I couldn't stay the wide-eyed ingenue for ever.'

'Why not? I liked her. She was honest and straightforward and a man knew where he was with her.'

Poor Martin. Didn't he realise that if they'd fallen in love it couldn't have been like that? Despite his seniority, she suddenly felt older and wiser than he was. She knew that being honest and straightforward and knowing exactly where you stand with each other is what friendship is all about. Love, especially the vulnerable early stages of falling into it, is a much more complex relationship. For her own protection a girl has to throw up so many smokescreens that it's a wonder the man ever manages to pierce the murk and find her.

'Oh, Martin,' she said, and on impulse she reached across the table and squeezed his hand.

Instead of squeezing her hand back and letting go, he held on to it and carried it up to his lips. Her index finger was selected for his kiss, then very meaningfully he placed the favoured finger against her cheek in the manner of transferring the kiss there.

Her pulse acknowledged that it was a very sensual thing to do.

His eyes fixed on hers in a full-beamed hold. They were gently provocative. 'That's all I wanted to know. Your manner has been putting up "Don't touch" signs. Wouldn't you say that's just torn them down? You're not indifferent to me, after all.'

'I responded to a trick. It was a new experience . . .' She wavered to a stop.

'And who says old friends can't share new experiences?'

She shook her head. Her voice was gentle. 'Count this old friend out, Martin. For us it would be too dangerous. We like each other too much. It would be fatally easy to mistake our feelings for something else.'

She wondered how bad a beating he had taken from Tara. When Sylvia told her they had split up, she had assumed it was by mutual consent. Now, if she was reading Martin right, it would appear that Tara had been the one to call it a day. Martin was bruised. She hoped his ego had taken the worst of it. She could put balm on his ego without being false to herself, but she couldn't heal his heart. That finger-tip trick had been an effective pulse-raiser. She would have had to be made of stone not to respond, but it had been pure sensualism that had left her heart untouched.

'I'm not suggesting we rush anything, Jan. The treatment Tara gave me would be enough to put some men off women for life. At the other extreme, I know it would be very easy, and comforting, to turn to someone on the rebound. I won't let it be you. I value our friendship too much to put it in jeopardy by making false claims. The fact that I find you a very exciting and attractive lady is not a false claim. It is also true to say that I've barely thought about Tara this evening, and I can't remember when I've enjoyed myself more. Do you know, I haven't felt this relaxed and as happy since we stopped going around together. So . . . all I'm saying is, let's not be too hasty. Can we be friends . . . and see what happens?'

'We are friends. Nothing has altered that.'

'Don't look so frightened, Jan. I've learnt my lesson. I won't hurt you again.'

'I'm not thinking of myself. I don't want to hurt you. That's why I've got to impress on you that friendship is all that's on offer.'

He was neither perturbed, nor put off. 'You seem to forget, Jan, that I've always liked a challenge.'

She consoled herself with the thought that she had tried to get through to him.

On the short drive home, the mood reverted back to the easy Martin-and-Jan camaraderie.

At her door it came naturally to say:

'Coming in for a cup of coffee?'

'Yes please.'

In the old days, many an enjoyable evening had been wound up in the cosy atmosphere of her mother's kitchen. Although she had sophisticatedly asked him in for coffee, her hand reached out automatically for the cocoa tin. As he had done countless times before, Martin raided the pantry and pounced on the green and cream cake tin which had never let him down in the past, and didn't fail him now.

'Your mother must have known I was coming. She's baked my favourite fruit cake.'

'Don't be so conceited!' Her smile softened the rebuke. 'It's a good keeping cake and she probably made it so that she'd have some sweet stuff in for when they return.'

'I didn't know they were away,' he said, taking up the kitchen knife and cutting generously. 'Your mother won't begrudge me a piece. Where have they gone?'

'I was going to ask you if you knew.'

'Your mother can certainly cook. She's going to make some man a wonderful mother-in-law. I don't know where they've gone because I haven't been in touch with your parents very much lately. But that's an omission I intend to rectify. This is comfortable, Jan.'

Too comfortable. The kitchen was at the back of the house and private from prying eyes. Jan jumped up briskly and led the way through into the lounge, making the excuse of wanting to put a record on. Deliberately she did not close the curtains.

She chose a single player which they both liked, and when the little arm clicked back to base she said: 'It's late. Finish your cocoa and go home.'

'You're very obvious, Jan. Do you honestly think leaving the curtains open is going to put me off? Anyway, I like giving nosey passers-by something to talk about.'

Jan sat rooted in her chair, holding the cocoa mug in front of her as though it would afford protection. The cocoa mug was taken from her and placed on a side table. Martin picked her up out of the chair, moulded her to his body in the closest hug she'd ever known, and proceeded to kiss her.

He had always kissed her goodnight when they'd spent an evening together, but never like this. His mouth was hard and passionate and bruised her lips. It was the searing flame, without the qualifying tenderness. And these rough, exploring hands in no way related to the gentleness she had come to expect from Martin. At first she thought he had lost control, but then she realised he was avenging himself for the wrong that Tara had done to him. It was something, an excitable fury, he needed to get out of his system, and Jan knew instinctively that if she put up a struggle it would take longer for it to burn out.

He let her go so abruptly that she almost keeled over. Yet as she saw the stricken look come to his eye, her determination to stand by him and help him was staunch. The years of their friendship rallied to her aid and she lifted her hand to touch his cheek. 'Don't say a word. I understand.'

'Dearest Jan,' he said brokenly. 'I wish I did.'

For the second time that evening he touched his lips to her hand. But this time it was not a trick to inflame her senses, but a gesture of abject apology. The contrasting gentleness after his recent brutality brought the tears to her eyes.

'Goodnight, Martin,' she said.

She leaned limply against the door she had closed behind him, listened for the sound of his car driving off, and then shot home the bolt.

Feeling emotionally spent, she started up the stairs. Her trembly legs had only taken her half way, when she heard the knock on the door. What had brought Martin back? She couldn't face him again this evening. It was asking too much of her.

The knock sounded again. Martin knew she was in. Of course she must answer the door to him.

But when she drew back the bolt and opened the door, it wasn't Martin she faced. It was, incredibly, David glowering down at her.

'May I come in?' he enquired with a sardonic lift of one dark eyebrow when it became apparent she wasn't going to do the niceties without being prompted.

'Of course. Please do.' She stood aside to let him enter and then guided him into the lounge, flicking on light switches as she went.

The heavy velvet curtains were still undrawn.

'With your permission, I'll close these.' Without waiting for the former, he did the latter. 'Much better. I hate to feel that someone out there could be looking in.'

Jan met his eyes squarely, but it was still only a tentative thought in her mind that David had looked in on her and Martin. She could tell nothing from his expression.

'This letter arrived for you shortly after you left.'

She looked down at the envelope which he had taken from his pocket and placed in her hand. She recognised her mother's handwriting.

'You didn't come all this way to play postman,' she said, trying to shake her brain free of its stultifying numbness.

'No. I had another reason.'

Whatever that might be, he had travelled a fair distance and her curiosity must wait until certain formalities were got out of the way.

'I'll make you a cup of tea. And something to eat. You must be hungry after your

84

journey.'

'Thank you, that's most thoughtful, but unnecessary. I arrived quite a bit earlier. You weren't in, so I thought I might as well kill a bit of time by going out for a meal.'

His brusque manner was beginning to set her teeth on edge. 'I'm sorry you had a tedious wait.'

The sarcastic inflection in her voice did not go unnoticed and was acknowledged in the supercilious lift of an eyebrow. 'Did I give that impression? I have spent a most delightful and diverting evening in the company of a young lady of your acquaintance. She was on the doorstep when I got here. Apparently she was there at your invitation. An amazingly tolerant and good-natured girl, I thought. I wouldn't have been so nice if I'd been ditched because a more attractive proposition cropped up.'

A girl would have a hard task to find a more attractive proposition than this cool, arrogant, unfairly handsome man. But that wasn't the issue.

'Someone waiting here, you say? Now who could that be?'

'Did you stand up more than one person?'

'I didn't stand anybody up.' Why did he always put her in the wrong? 'If you mean Sylvia Friers, I didn't ask her round, she invited herself.'

'And so you felt justified in being out when she came. Weren't you just a little concerned

85

that she was trailing all that way for nothing?'

'But it wasn't for nothing, was it?' Jan said obstreperously. 'She got you.' And if she knew Sylvia, she thought bitterly, she would make the most of it. 'You two should have got along famously. You are so alike.'

'Knowing your opinion of me, that is hardly complimentary to your friend. Shame on you, Jan. She spoke glowingly of you.'

Jan hissed sharply: 'She would.' It was infuriating and laughable, but in this man's presence her temper was set permanently at flash-point. The moment he entered the room she was in, her sweet and placid nature flew out of the window and she said all manner of nasty uncharitable things that were completely out of character.

With immaculate calm he said: 'If you mutilate that letter much more, you won't be able to read it.'

'It's from my mother,' she said.

'Oh lord. I'd forgotten you had parents.' His lovely calm had received a sharp jolt. His eyes swept up to the ceiling. 'I can understand your not being in a great hurry to read it because you'll have caught up with all the news. I am urgently reminded of the fact that at any moment an irate father could burst in, demanding an explanation.'

'An explanation? I'm sorry, I don't know what you mean.'

'Well, we have been kicking up a bit of a

rumpus, so he might come down initially to complain about the noise. Then he will take one look at you, and as fathers of daughters are said to be biased, he'll link your raging temper with your dishevelled appearance and arrive at the natural conclusion that you put up a fight. And from what I saw, you weren't objecting. If you had been, I would have moved in pretty quickly and taken it out of his hide.'

So he had seen. Trust him to arrive at the crucial moment. His reaction was startling. Would he really have come to her defence? His interpretation of the scene was less pleasing, but predictable. She had let Martin paw her for the most praiseworthy of reasons. But to an onlooker it would have seemed grubby and sordid.

'It wasn't as it looked, David.'

'I'm not questioning your boyfriend's right to take liberties. I'm merely saying . . .'

'He's not my boyfriend, at least he was but he isn't any more. And he wasn't taking liberties, at least he was, but it wasn't . . . Oh, what's the use! I can't explain and even if I could you wouldn't understand because you know nothing about standing by people when they've been knocked to the ground, and friendship and loyalties, and understanding them when they go off course.'

'I wasn't going to lecture you. I haven't the right to. I was attempting to point out that

87

your father is going to look at you, and I'm going to get the blame. In which case,' he said sadly, 'his opinion of me would just about coincide with yours.'

She regretted being so brutal to him. It would have helped if he'd lashed a few angry words back at her . . . instead of looking at her with eyes of hurt.

She gulped and challenged: 'Have you ever given me cause to have a better opinion of you?'

'I reckon not.'

'And you're not about to rectify that?'

'You ask an awful lot of questions, Jan. May I ask one?'

'What is it?'

'Do you think that anything I could say would reform your opinion of me?'

'According to Linda, yes.'

'But at the back of your mind you think Linda is biased, don't you? I mean *you*, what do *you* think?'

'I don't know.'

And then she did something totally unexpected. She raised up on tiptoe and with total deliberation and absorption, she kissed him on the mouth. His arms started to come up and for a moment she thought he was going to return her tender impulse, but he must have changed his mind because his arms returned to his sides. Feeling rebuffed, her chin dropped in acute embarrassment. Apparently, her mother's letter had fallen from her hand and she saw it looking up at her from the carpet. She swooped down to retrieve it and, glad for something to do, tore open the envelope and tried to bring into focus her mother's large script which blurred before the silly moistness in her eyes. Even though she was inwardly quaking, her fingers were remarkably steady and didn't give her away.

She hoped, if David thought anything, that he would think she was a slow reader.

At length she said with what she hoped would pass for a laugh, 'My parents have gone to stay with some friends. Listen to this bit of irony. In her letter my mother says that when they get back at the end of this week, she hopes I might find the time to pay a visit home.'

'You mean they're not in bed?'

'No. I'm here by myself.'

'Nice to know that somebody's on my side in something. I'm glad I don't have to face your father. At least not just at this moment. How long will it take you to pack your suitcase?'

'Sorry?'

'Don't be so exasperating. You must know I've come to fetch you back.'

'That's a bit cheeky. After that demonstration of absurd male reasoning. How am I supposed to know?'

'Because it's obvious. You surely didn't think I came all this way for the dubious pleasure of quarrelling with you?'

'Why?' she said, and saw his expression flicker to disbelief then back to irritation. 'I don't mean why is it obvious,' she said with a touch of irritation of her own, 'I've decided to let that one pass. I mean why have you come to fetch me?'

His expression now inclined to sheepishness. His voice was wry. 'I'll grant you the last laugh. I hadn't reckoned with Stephanie, had I? I must hand it to your sex. At a very early age you discover the importance of sticking together. When she discovered that you'd gone, she started to scream her head off. She won't eat. When she's not screaming she's crying. When she's not screaming or crying, she's asleep.'

'Oh, my poor little pet. Where is she now? Who have you left her with?'

'I dumped her on Linda and Hugh. Hopefully she's tucked up and fast asleep in the spare bedroom. But knowing Stephanie, I can't guarantee that. Your poor little pet is one horribly spoilt brat.'

'According to you, I am responsible for spoiling her. If I'm so unsuitable, why come to take me back? We both know this tantrum of hers can only last so long. You've only to stand firm, and she would come round to the new order of things.'

'You don't take prisoners, do you? So you were right. I acted too hastily when I dismissed

90

you. It was too soon after losing her mother and yes, she was clinging to you as some sort of safe anchor. I still think children need authority to make them feel safe. All spoiling does is give them a false set of values and a feeling of insecurity. She'll come round to me. But right at this moment it's you she wants. How's that for grovelling? Does that satisfy you, or do you want me to go down on my knees and beg you to come back with me?'

'That won't be necessary. I'll get my things together.'

'No.' He touched her arm. 'On second thoughts, the morning will do. You look all in. Get a good night's sleep. We'll make a start straight after breakfast in the morning.'

Oh no! Please don't go tender on me, she thought. If you do, I'll cry, and we should both hate that.

'What about you? Where will you sleep?'

'Don't worry about me. I'll book into a hotel.'

'At this time of night? I'll make the bed up in the spare room.'

His smile was unaccustomedly boyish. 'I was hoping you'd say that. Oh, and . . . er . . . I'm sorry if I was a bit frosty earlier on.'

Perhaps he'd been hanging about outside longer than she'd imagined. He could have been sitting in one of the parked cars. When you are waiting for someone, five minutes can seem like an hour.

'That's all right,' she said generously. 'I can understand why.'

What could she possibly have said wrong in that? she wondered as she saw the frost forming again.

'Good grief! You can't believe that. That's the most absurd thing I've heard. I couldn't care less.'

'That's splendid. I don't know what you're going on about. I was expressing sympathy in case you'd had a long wait. And now I'll go and see about your bed.'

While she was about it, she hunted out a pair of her father's pyjamas.

She flung them at him. 'As my father is about six inches smaller than you are, they'll look a bit ludicrous. You can take them or leave them.'

'I'll leave them, thank you.' A renegade twinkle came to his eye. 'Remember to knock when you bring in my early morning tea.'

CHAPTER FOUR

Curled up in bed, only her body quiescent, her thoughts were racing. It hadn't been easy for David to come for her and as he said, the last laugh was hers. Only she didn't feel like laughing.

She was roused by someone shaking her

shoulder.

'Come on, Jan! Wake up, won't you!'

She didn't want to wake up. In her dream David was bending over her, calling her name with such sweet urgency, and she didn't want to snap back to reality.

She opened her eyes, and it really was David bending over her.

'What's the matter?' she said, struggling up on to her elbow.

'Are you expecting anybody?'

'No.'

'I've news for you. You've got visitors. A blue car has just pulled up, and a grey-haired man and a small, fairish woman have just got out of it.'

'Mum and Dad.'

'With my luck, that's exactly what I expected you to say.' He wore the same shirt and trousers he had worn last night, but he looked less debonair without the jacket and with an unshaven chin. 'I'll go and put a tie on for the hanging,' he said.

She collapsed back on to her pillow in a fit of giggles. 'Don't look so worried, David. I'll have a word with Dad. And if all else fails, you're bigger than he is.'

'Thank you for nothing. No girl is going to speak up for me. I'll square it with Dad myself. There is something you could do for me, though.'

'And what would that be?'

'Could you manage to look about twelve years old?'

Jan had always known what particularly nice parents she had and that she held a very special place in their hearts. Their trust in her was endorsed by their unruffled acceptance of David's presence, *before* David put them in the picture.

They accepted the sacking and the urgent reinstatement as a matter of course. Her mother spoke for both of them when she said it was lucky they'd had to come back earlier than intended. Not so lucky for their friends because a small domestic crisis had made it necessary. 'Their eldest son is wrestling with a new marriage and Mum has been sent for to act as mediator. I think she's making a mistake in going, young people should sort it out themselves, but that's beside the point. It's given us the chance to see Jan, even if briefly, and more important still, the opportunity of meeting you, Professor Spedding.'

It had been dawning on Jan for some minutes that her parents, her father in particular, had recognised David from somewhere and—well—seemed to be deferring to him almost as if he was somebody special.

Her father confirmed this by saying: 'I didn't realise that Jan's employer was *the* David Spedding. I saw you on television a good while back, two years ago and probably

94

nearer three, and I was most impressed by your views and—what shall I call it?—a certain outspokenness. You must find your work extremely rewarding. It must be gratifying to know that what you are finding out today will benefit the general public tomorrow.'

'I'm afraid my particular field of research has more hazards than high spots. But I like what I'm doing, and it's a lucky man who can say that.'

'Yes, indeed, Professor Spedding.'

David tugged at his ear. 'Do you think you can both call me David?'

Her father replied earnestly: 'I think we can manage that. But you must return the compliment. We'd like to be Muriel and John to you. That right, my love?'

'Yes.' Two dimples found their way into the smile her mother gave David. 'We're a family without formalities. Can I get you another cup of tea, David?'

'Yes please, Muriel.' David's return smile told Jan that he was as enchanted with her mother as she was with him. 'Jan.'

His voice broke through her thoughts. 'Sorry, what was it, David?'

'I was just saying that if you've finished your breakfast, you ought to see about packing your suitcase. We don't want to be late.'

Parental eyebrows that had not so much as quavered over events which could not by any stretch of the imagination be called everyday, lifted at the speed with which she went to do his bidding. Oh well, it was too late to slow her step now.

When she came downstairs again, it was to find her mother flitting between the dining room and the kitchen, straightening and tidying and generally putting her house back in order.

'Where are David and Dad?'

'In the lounge. No, you mustn't join them. Your father wants to say something to David.'

Jan didn't like the sound of that. 'What about?'

'I don't know, dear.'

'I hope Dad isn't being silly.'

'Funny, that's what he says about you.'

'It's just a job, Mum.'

'One that doesn't require your hard-earned qualifications.'

'I'd wondered what you thought about that.'

'Education is never wasted. I'm well aware that you went after the job as a temporary measure to get over a sticky patch. You didn't count on your heart getting committed. I mean, of course,' she said, levelling her daughter a shrewd look, 'to Stephanie. Poor little mite. I wouldn't think much of you if you didn't want to stand by her until she got over it. Is that roughly it?'

'That's exactly it.'

What a wise mother she'd got. Sympathetic and understanding. Sometimes too understanding,

Jan thought, remembering that shrewd look.

* * *

'You're lucky in your parents, Jan,' David remarked as they got under way.

'I know. They are two of the nicest, if not *the* nicest people I know. They certainly took a liking to you.'

'It's generous of you to admit it, all except your "I wonder why?" tone.'

'I'd like to know what Dad said to you.'

'I know you would.'

'Do you have to be so infuriatingly mysterious?'

'At least it makes a change,' he said blandly. 'Most of the time you find me plain infuriating.'

'My father seems to respect you an awful lot.'

'That's more than can be said of his daughter.'

'Are you very important in your job?' Jan asked, following her own line of enquiry.

'You favour your father most in looks, but you've got your mother's charming nose and her vivacity. Who do you get your tenacity from?'

'Whoever I get it from, it isn't doing me much good. You could give lessons to a clam.'

He laughed, and announced out of the blue, 'I've got plans to extend Larkspur Cottage.'

'How?'

'I've bought the cottage next door.'

'That's quick work.'

'No it isn't. I've been negotiating, through Ralph, to purchase it for some time, but the deal has only just been closed. I'm now having plans drawn up to knock the two cottages into one to make a decent sized place to live in.'

'You intend to settle in Willowbridge then?'

'Why shouldn't I?' he challenged.

'No reason. In your place, I'd want to go somewhere where I was liked.'

'Be driven out, you mean? No way. It's perfectly located, near enough to my work, but just far enough away to make it the perfect retreat from the scourges of the day. Idyllic in summer, cosy in winter. I intend to keep the old look of the place, the oak beams and all that, but a few discreet and tasteful modernisations won't come amiss, like a shower unit and a new bathroom. And those little peep-holes they call windows might look old-world, but they don't do a thing for me. They've got to go.'

'Oh yes!' Jan said, catching his enthusiasm. It was one of her pet grievances that the view was wasted.

'And you know the outbuilding? Mrs. Weaver turned it to good use for her constant stream of visitors. That will come in most useful. Long term, I need a quiet retreat where I can work. Just for now it will double as a bedroom for me. That will release a bedroom in the cottage for visitors.'

While Linda had been staying he had given his bed up for her and made do with the sofa.

'Did Linda mind having Stephanie dumped on her?' she asked.

'Linda always likes to have a little grumble at first, just to make sure she isn't being taken for granted, but she can always be relied on to help out.'

'I'm looking forward to meeting Hugh.'

'I'm afraid you're not going to. Not this trip, anyway. When I left their house, Hugh was on the point of departing on a lecture tour.'

'How far are we off now?'

'About an hour's drive.'

Because of a later start than anticipated, they didn't arrive until mid-afternoon.

Stephanie had been having a dressing-up session. She paraded precariously forward to meet them in one of Linda's dresses, its voluminous skirt extravagantly tucked into a belt at the waist. She wore a picture hat that dipped saucily to eyes of green merriment under a subtle dusting of eye-shadow in Mother Nature's softest moss green. Her pert little nose nestled under a light toasting of beige foundation. Her normally pink cheeks were a tint pinker with blusher, and fashion's brightest poppy red lipstick glistened her upward turned little mouth. In Linda's ankle-breaking spiky heeled sandals, ten little toes, with colour matched poppy red toenails, wriggled importantly to be noticed.

'Who is this exotic creature?' Jan said in delighted awe that was not made up entirely of pretence. Linda's hand was behind the transformation and she knew her stuff. 'Won't someone introduce us?'

Stephanie squealed in joy.

'This is Her Serene Highness, the Princess Stephanie, who has crossed many oceans to favour our fair land,' Linda announced.

'Your Highness,' said Jan, sweeping to the floor in a deep curtsy.

Stephanie's little face was ecstatic; David's less so.

'Look at my darling David,' Linda said, drawing attention to his sombre expression. 'He doesn't approve.' She didn't wag her finger at him, but had she done so the tone of voice she used would have been a fitting accompaniment. 'Let me tell you this, my lad, it diverted Stephanie, which is more than you achieved. And it preserved my sanity. I was at my wits' end, having exhausted my repertoire of nursery rhymes. The cow is weary of jumping over the moon, and Polly has lost count of how many times she's put the kettle on. Which reminds me. Nice cup of tea? And something to eat? How hungry are you?'

'Tatty Bear's very hungry,' said Stephanie.

'I'm glad to hear it,' Linda replied. 'He's been on a starvation diet, even though I've tempted him with pink blancmange and his favourite orange cream chocolate biscuits. Tatty Bear's been ever so miserable.'

'Tatty Bear isn't miswerable now,' said Stephanie.

'I didn't think he would be. It will be all smiles now that your beloved Jan is back.' Linda's eyes seemed to stretch enquiringly to David, but he was looking the other way.

Despite what Linda said, Stephanie didn't fuss round Jan, and even went to the other extreme of practically ignoring her, and Jan knew she was being punished for going away. But it was no coincidence that the plump baby fingers were no longer tied in angry knots, and the roaring unanswerable animal that had filled her and tore at her and crushed everybody around her into a state of distressed inadequacy, was magically appeased.

'Jan was saying she was looking forward to meeting Hugh. Pity he's away,' David said.

'I was just thinking the same myself.' Linda's face brightened. 'I know! Hugh will be back on Friday. Why don't you all stay and keep me company, and then Jan can meet him. I can put you up. No trouble, honestly.'

'Count me out,' David said. 'I've got an appointment tomorrow with the Planning Officer about the alterations to the cottage.'

'That's no excuse,' Linda declared. 'We don't live all that far away. You could keep your appointment from here.'

'I could, but I'm not. I don't have to wait for planning permission to get cracking on the outbuilding. I'm going home to start on that. How about a compromise? Jan and Stephanie could stay on.'

'That's even better,' Linda said with a jaunty lift of her chin. 'We can have an "all girls together". Will you collect your two to take them back home, or shall I deliver?'

David not only took the point, he even went as far as to emphasise it. 'Either way. I can collect *my two*, or leave you to run them home.'

'You collect, then,' Linda said emphatically. 'That's the right way. A man should pander to his womenfolk,' she added mischievously.

David's eyes were not without amusement. 'I pander to you, Linda Liberty Taker.'

'You don't, you know. I admit to taking the liberty of giving unsought-for advice, but I might as well save my breath because you never take it.'

'Ah, but there's a very good reason for that. Your advice so rarely coincides with my wishes.'

'In other words you'll do as you like even though what you like isn't always good for you. I don't know why I bother.' But as she looked at her godson it was plain to see that her exasperation was tempered by her deep affection.

*　　*　　*

As they walked back up the drive after seeing David off, Linda said: 'I'll show you round the house now. You'll notice the décor is personality-matched to me, which is how it should be. A woman spends more time in the home than a man does. And, anyway, Hugh's sense of colour isn't as good as mine. He let me have a completely free hand, and having had a preview of his taste, I took it. Except for his own private sanctum, his study. Go in while you may,' she said throwing open the door. 'But do remember that it's forbidden territory when Hugh is at home.'

Not only did Jan see what Linda meant, she thought she had been quite kind over the matter of Hugh's tawdry choice in colours. In fairness, the same colours in muted shades could have looked all right, and time might have the same effect of dulling and blending. But in its newly decorated spanking clean form the bright biscuit ceiling did not go with the shrieking yellow doors. And the tiny square patterned wallpaper did not marry itself to the large cabbage roses spattered on the carpet.

'Hugh only has one claim of good taste to his credit, bless him,' said Linda, closing the door firmly behind them, 'and that was in choosing me. If he did,' she amended wistfully. 'Sometimes I think life chooses our partners for us. It's just a question of being in the right

103

place at the right time, and not being too stubborn to see it.' Jan was rather sorry that Stephanie had run on ahead and was out of earshot, because then Linda wouldn't have been able to say, 'Why can't David see it? Stubborn as he is he must see that to marry you would be the perfect solution all round.'

'Do you mind!' Jan covered her embarrassment with a lightness she did not feel, and at the same time voiced a truth. 'I don't want to be a perfect solution.'

'Oh, lord, no! Of course you wouldn't be. I worded it awkwardly. I shouldn't have said anything at all about David marrying you, but wishful-thinking-out-loud has always been my downfall, although it once turned out to be my advantage. It was my saying something much like that to Hugh which prompted him to propose to me.' She smiled. 'I can see you don't believe me, but it's true. It goes without saying that this is the kitchen,' she said, opening another door.

The lounge, where all the shades of green, mixed like Mother Nature does in the woodlands, the ideal backing for the smooth uncluttered lines of the pine furniture, had already been inspected and delighted over. So it was upstairs for bedroom inspection.

Linda and Hugh's room was large and elegant. By this time they had caught up with Stephanie who was entranced by the long cheval mirror and had to be dragged to the next room which was hers, with an appropriate ballerina-patterned wallpaper. Next door to that was Jan's room. Lots of white and cool restful jade, with a warming of pink in the curtains gently wafting at the open window.

When it was time for Stephanie to be tucked up for the night, she turned her cheek away from Jan's goodnight kiss, but although she wasn't quite ready to forgive Jan, she didn't sob into her pillow and within minutes she had dropped into a contented sleep.

'Peace, perfect peace,' said Linda.

It was shattered by the ringing of the telephone.

It turned out to be Hugh.

Returning to the lounge, Linda said: 'He always makes the time to phone me to say goodnight.' Her features wore a contented glow.

It prompted Jan to ask: 'Do you ever regret not meeting him when you were younger?'

'Good heavens no! I don't feel my age, and I know I don't look it, and that's not entirely due to luck, either. A young mind can retard the aging process. The taking years are now behind me. Know what I mean by that? No? Well, the taking years find out what you are really made of. Every day takes something from you, but it's fair, because it gives it back in knowledge. Life can deliver some hard knocks, but it gives you the resilience to deal with them. Hugh wouldn't have liked the "before" me as much as he likes the "after" me. He would have detested the ambitious, opinionated person I was; he adores the warm, wise, fulfilled woman I am.'

It was the word fulfilled that played on Jan's mind. She just stopped short of a great impertinence, realising it could also be a source of great hurt, by not asking Linda if she regretted not having had children.

As if answering her thoughts, Linda said: 'Hugh would have made a wonderful father. He dotes on children. But he's much too intelligent to wallow in that sort of unprofitable "if only it could have been" nonsense. As for me, I honestly don't know. I've never decided whether I'm not maternal enough, or too maternal. I could never have been a part-time mother. I would have had to give up my work and devote myself wholeheartedly to my children, but I would have felt cheated and bitterly denied if I hadn't had my career. It was a lucky day for me when Hugh came into my life and I swept him off his feet. He thinks it was the other way round and I'm wise enough not to disillusion him and let him go on thinking he did the sweeping.' Her happy mood restored, she gave Jan a long twinkling look. 'You could crack it with David, if you wanted to. He wouldn't know what had hit him. Why don't you let me do you over, Jan? You're an incredibly pretty girl. With just a whisper of help, a slightly more sophisticated hairstyle, a smudge of eyeshadow to bring into play the true loveliness of your eyes by deepening the colour of your irises, you could be a ravishing beauty.'

'I don't want to ravish.' Pride and humour were gently balanced in Jan's eyes. 'It wouldn't seem honest. If ever I do crack it with David, I'll do it off my own bat and by being me. But thank you for the offer. It's appreciated.'

'I'd appreciate it if instead of dismissing it out of hand you'd bear it in mind for possible future reference. Remember, if ever you change your mind, help is at the other end of a telephone.'

Jan said, 'Thank you,' knowing she would never call on Linda for this sort of help. To change the subject she said: 'Did you know it was in David's mind to buy the cottage next door?'

'Oh yes. He began negotiating the deal while Annabel was still alive, because he thought that two adjacent cottages would be a better investment than just the one. That, of course, was long before he got the idea of knocking the two cottages into one to make a sumptuous home for himself.'

Linda had voiced what had never been put into words but which Jan had always felt, that David had never intended to live at Larkspur Cottage with Annabel. But there was a point here that demanded to be queried.

'Investment? Isn't that an odd term to use?'

107

Linda replied unwarily with an inflection of surprise in her voice: 'What's odd about that? Why else would he buy a house for Annabel to live in?'

Jan found herself gasping in disbelief. 'I should have thought because she was his wife.'

Linda looked helpless as she attempted to keep a cool head and a low profile.

Jan leapt into the pause this hesitation created. 'I'll grant that they never lived together as man and wife, but she was his wife and so he was surely obligated to house her?'

Linda lifted her eyes to Jan's. She spoke very clearly and with a dogged determination that forbad interruption. 'You've achieved the rare distinction of putting me on the spot. I'd dearly love to argue the ethics of the situation with you, Jan, but I can't. My tongue is tied by my stupid loyalty to David, even though I consider him to be a quixotic fool. I had wondered, but I couldn't be sure. However, it now seems obvious that he hasn't been as forthcoming about his affairs as I have been about mine. I'm not ducking the issue, I'm merely saying the decision to talk or not to talk is a very private thing and that it is, and must remain, David's business.'

'I didn't mean to pry,' Jan said in a penitent voice.

'I know you didn't.' Linda's eyes were warm and understanding. 'Shall we see if there's anything worth watching on television?'

Linda was the perfect hostess, with an amazing insight into what little girls like to do best. She dreamed up so many interesting, diverting things to do that the time passed with unbelievable speed.

Tatty Bear managed to be reasonably good. He didn't fall in the river on the afternoon they went boating. He didn't get up to any truly naughty pranks, and only committed slight misdemeanours, like spilling Stephanie's glass of milk all over Linda's clean tablecloth. It would have been a very relaxing break if Jan could have chased away the 'accident waiting to happen' feeling. When the worst happened, it didn't help that she felt it was her fault because of her lack of vigilance.

It was Friday. David had phoned to say he was on the point of leaving and would be with them very soon. Stephanie was playing in the sun-drenched garden, a flitting butterfly in her yellow dress, if lacking its delicacy and lightness as her feet trampled Linda's vegetable patch. Inside, Linda and Jan were enjoying the quiet of the lounge, and a companionable chat over a cup of coffee, when both their heads shot up.

Linda identified the noise that had shattered the peace. 'Breaking glass.' And they both unfroze and started to run.

'Look what naughty Tatty Bear has done,' said Stephanie, pointing to the upturned handle of the garden rake, resting at a most peculiar angle in the cold frame.

'Take a deep breath, Jan,' Linda's voice urged. 'It helps. And bear in mind that it could have been worse. It could have been the greenhouse.'

'That's the trouble, Linda, I bear too many things in mind. It's a point of contention between me and David that by not punishing Stephanie I'm turning her into a spoilt child. I agree there's nothing more unlovable than that, but how can you punish a child who has been so punished by life?'

'It does add to the problem,' a deeper voice than Linda was capable of producing admitted, 'but the circumstances you are in sympathy with make it imperative not to shelve it. Children, even those as young as Stephanie, soon pick up what tune to play. Sympathise if you must, but don't let it show. And kindly move out of the way. If you can't act, I will. I won't stand by and see a sweet child completely ruined.'

'David!' As Jan swung round to face him, her chin went up. He'd picked his moment to arrive, she thought dolefully. 'If you must punish someone, let it be me. I'm the one to blame for leaving Stephanie to her own devices for too long.'

'I might just take you up on that later. For

the moment, you will have to wait. To be effective on a child, the medicine's got to be immediate. Now, out of my way before I put you out.'

Jan knew she couldn't block him for ever; she'd thought to stand in front of him to deter him long enough for his temper to subside. Only, as usual, she was the one in a temper. David was cool and enviably calm as he picked her up, put her out of the way, and went charging after Stephanie who hadn't lingered long enough to hear any of this adult conversation and was hiding somewhere in the tangle of weeds that Linda hadn't got round to clearing.

He came back with his fingers wrapped round Stephanie's wrist. Little fingers know how to wriggle free, wrists don't. He looked mountainous beside her diminutive figure.

'Not my fault,' Stephanie hiccuped mutinously. 'Tatty Bear did it.'

'You are sticking to that?'

'Tatty Bear did it,' she repeated tearfully.

'Then Tatty Bear will be punished, not you.'

Jan had absolutely no idea what was coming. In a moment of wild and stupid relief, she actually thought that David had sought a diplomatic way round the problem. Tatty Bear could take a slapped leg, and Stephanie would be on hand to comfort and kiss the disciplined toy bear better.

To her horror she heard David say: 'Garden

rakes must not be thrown into cold frames. It's solitary confinement for Tatty Bear. That will give him time to think about his naughtiness.'

'If you forgive him this time, I'm quite sure Tatty Bear won't do anything as naughty again,' Jan interjected.

Ignoring her, David said: 'Linda, may I borrow Hugh's study for the purpose?'

Looking every bit as anguished as Jan felt, Linda nodded helplessly.

As she explained to Jan afterwards, what else could she do? Everybody had been too lax with Stephanie and she was getting completely out of hand, and she couldn't undermine David's authority as he seemed to be the only one capable of straightening her out. And the punishment did fit the crime. Stephanie couldn't sail through life getting away with murder by blaming Tatty Bear for her misdeeds. Deprivation of her beloved toy would make her think twice next time.

But he was more than a toy. He was her comfort and her solace, her confidant and even the sponge for her tears. It was cruel of David to shut him away from her in the forbidden bounds of Hugh's study.

And yet she didn't know why she was surprised. His cavalier treatment of Annabel had told her what an inhuman beast he was. Well, her attitude towards him might have softened for a while, but that was fragile history now. She was on her guard, and she

112

would make sure she didn't weaken again, not even if he tugged his ear right off in that little-boy habit of his when he was unsure of his ground or embarrassed.

On the principle of what can't be cured must be endured, Jan buckled down and told a red-eyed, sulky-mouthed Stephanie a made-up story about a foolish little bear who had been very naughty, but who turned out to be a brave little bear who took his punishment on the snout with the courage of a lion.

One blessing. Jan was relieved of the unpleasant necessity of having to make polite conversation with David by his insistence on making good the damage. He disappeared into the garden to measure up, and then went into town to buy the replacement panes of glass, and was busily employed fitting them into the cold frame.

The telephone rang and Jan heard Linda say: 'Oh no, Hugh! Of all the times to be delayed. What's that? A snag? You think David might be able to help? Yes, he's here. Hang on a moment.' Linda turned round and said to Jan: 'Did you catch that? Hugh wants a word with David. Be a love and give him a shout for me, will you? I might as well talk to Hugh until he comes.'

Jan couldn't very well refuse. She found David totally absorbed in his task. He'd cleared away the broken glass and had already fitted one new pane in. She hadn't visualised him in the role of handyman and was surprised to see he was making quite a competent job of it.

'Hugh is on the phone. He wants to speak to you,' she said stiffly.

He didn't tug his ear; he just looked grim. 'I'll come right away.' He straightened up and wiped his hands on his handkerchief. It wasn't just grime he transferred, but a spreading circle of blood.

'You've hurt yourself!' she gasped, her heart taking a giant leap into her eyes.

'It's only a scratch.'

'See you clean it up,' she said briskly collecting herself, 'to save the risk of infection.'

'I will. Nice to know you care.'

'Care? I don't care. I was taken by surprise that's all. I didn't think werewolves bled.'

David turned on his heel without saying a word. With a haughty walk, Jan followed him into the house.

David could help, and so Hugh safely promised to be with them in time for dinner.

There was no question of their going before Hugh arrived as the whole point of her stay had been to meet him, but Jan realised they were going to have to keep Stephanie up long past her normal bedtime to make the homeward journey.

'You must stay for dinner,' Linda said. 'It seems a bit silly to dash off straight afterwards, so why don't you make the weekend of it?'

David made noises of disinclination, which Linda brushed away, and a compromise was arrived at. They would stay the night and travel the short distance home the following day.

'That's wonderful,' said Linda, but she added with a doubtful smile: 'The problem is, Hugh and I didn't intend to eat in. We've got a table booked at Danielle's Den. Danielle really is the name of the proprietress, Jan, and what she doesn't know about cuisine isn't worth knowing. Why don't I phone her and make it a reservation for four?'

'For three,' Jan said. 'I'll stay here with a sandwich on a tray and listen out for Stephanie.' She was glad of the excuse because she could think of nothing worse than a cosy foursome if David was to be one of the party.

'I hadn't forgotten Stephanie. There's a Mrs. Miller who lives two doors away whom I know would be happy to come and sit for her.'

'I honestly don't mind,' Jan insisted.

'But I do,' Linda said, equally insistent. 'I wouldn't dream of going out and enjoying myself and leaving you all alone. If you stay, then we all stay. I'll phone Danielle and cancel.'

Jan knew that Linda meant well. She thought that a night out in convivial surroundings would lighten the atmosphere between her and David. Jan also knew that kind-hearted Linda wouldn't enjoy herself if she thought that Jan was left behind to mope. She was over a barrel and she knew it.

With as much grace as she could muster, she said: 'All right. If Mrs. Miller will accommodate.'

David's quick frown could have meant either, or both, of two things. Her enthusiasm was so markedly lacking that it wouldn't have fooled anyone, and certainly not someone as astute as Linda. Or, he was equally unenthusiastic and had counted on her to get him out.

*   *   *

Hugh was very much as Jan imagined him to be. Big, genial, vague, lovable. He obviously adored Linda.

'Hello, Jan,' he said. 'Thank you for staying and keeping Linda company. It was kind of you.'

Jan replied with absolute truth: 'The kindness was Linda's for having me. She's given me a fabulous time.'

He smiled. 'We'll have chance to get better acquainted later.' He tapped his briefcase and sent a sheepish smile in Linda's direction. 'I must get the contents of this sewn up while it's still fresh in my mind. Don't worry, Linda, I know what time the table is booked for and I promise I won't make us late. David,' he said, his voice moving into crisp authority. 'Have

116

you a minute?'

*   *   *

Jan was ready to face the dreaded evening. Linda had once again offered her professional services, but Jan had declined. The hand that had floated the powder puff from her compressed all-in-one compact and applied a light film of coral lip gloss was her own. She knew it would show that it was her handiwork against Linda's immaculate make-up, but she didn't care. It didn't occur to her that youth has its own dazzle, and that her simple dress would make more elaborately gowned ladies shake their elegant heads in despair and wonder why they'd bothered.

It had been in Jan's mind to plunder Hugh's study and carry the confiscated bear back into Stephanie's loving arms, but Hugh and David were still in there, thwarting all opportunity.

When she went in to see Stephanie, she saw to her delight that the little girl was sleeping peacefully, her hair a golden halo on the pillow, one chubby hand crumpled under her cheek.

She was quietly retreating when the door opened to admit someone on a similar mission. The lemon light falling in at the door pinpointed David.

'She's asleep,' she whispered.

Instead of going straight out again, as she

expected, David said: 'I promise not to wake her,' and allowed Jan to slide out in front of him.

*   *   *

Two people out of four sending each other dark looks does not make an auspicious start to an evening. In truth, only Jan's eyes were dark and unfriendly, David's merely growled back.

The entrance to Danielle's Den was down a narrow flight of steps. The atmosphere was decidedly cellar-like; the prices kept it exclusive. In the corner a white, upright piano was being played by a slight, waif-like girl in a clinging white dress. She played tunes which Jan had never heard before and she wasn't surprised when Linda said they were her own compositions. She supplied her own vocal and her voice, though not strong, was prettily accented and pleasant to hear. Jan had no idea that the girl was Danielle, the proprietress, until much later. In the centre of the room a space had been cleared for dancing. The swift plunge into a Latin American tempo attracted only three couples, but as Danielle's expert fingers swept into a waltz-time melody, more couples drifted on to the floor.

'Would you like to dance?' David asked Jan.

'No thank you. I'm content to watch and listen.'

118

'I think you really want to dance, only you're too shy of getting up and attracting attention.'

'No, it's . . .'

But David had risen to his feet and the fingers enclosing her wrist, in the same inescapable hold he had used on Stephanie, forced her to do the same.

'You are dancing,' he said, his mouth close to her ear. 'Don't argue and don't make a scene.'

She was boiling, but there was nothing she could do but allow herself to be led forward and drawn into the circle of his arms.

'How dare you!' she gasped.

'I dare because I happen to be very fond of Linda and Hugh. I couldn't care less that you choose to spoil your own evening by behaving like an ungrateful, spoilt brat, but I will not have you ruining theirs. Hugh has been solidly immersed in work, and this is the first proper fun-break they've had in weeks. I wouldn't have stayed on and intruded only Linda insisted that she enjoyed your company, and in any case, I felt obliged to go into town for the glass to replace the damaged panes in the cold frame.'

'You don't have to go on. You've said more than enough. I didn't think. I also happen to be very fond of Linda. She's been on tenterhooks all day waiting for Hugh to come home, and I'm horrified at the thought of spoiling their evening.' She took a deep breath, and earned herself a look of quizzical amusement that dipped into grudging respect, as she trotted out in the manner of a child who has been thoughtless, but not deliberately cruel, 'Thank you for pulling me up about it. I promise to be good. Incidentally, you made an excellent job of the cold frame. I wasn't aware you had handyman inclinations.'

He threw back his head and laughed, and the robust sound attracted quite a few eyes to the tall, good-looking man and his sparkling eyed, bemused-faced partner. 'I have a number of inclinations that you don't know about. And I give grateful thanks that you don't.'

Because of David's plain speaking, it turned out to be a good evening. The meal, from the starter which did its job of flattering the tastebuds, to the aromatic coffee and orange scented liqueur, was memorable. And it wasn't just the taste. The steak Jan ordered was prepared and cooked at the table before her enchanted eyes, and that was an entertainment in itself. And not just for Jan. Her smile curved higher than the leaping flames, giving a new dimension of enjoyment to the more blasé diners around.

Towards the end of the evening, Danielle moved among the clientele, pausing at each table to ask its occupants if they had enjoyed their meal. She addressed people very correctly as Monsieur, Madame or Mademoiselle, but she called Linda, Hugh and David by name, and seemed to know them quite well. When it was Jan's turn, the petite French girl called her *chérie*, as if she appreciated her delight.

Warm as it was, there was a poignancy about Danielle's smile that made Jan shiver. She didn't know how or why, but she sensed a deep unhappiness. It was weird, but for a moment the shadows in the French girl's eyes put a blight on the evening and made her feel quite cold.

Soon after that they returned to Linda and Hugh's to dismiss a sleepy Mrs. Miller who said she hadn't heard a peep out of Stephanie.

Upstairs in her room, Jan undressed and got into bed, but not with the intention of going to sleep. She lay in the darkened room waiting for the house to settle down for the night. Hugh's heavier tread was the last to sound on the carpet outside her door. She waited for the click of his bedroom door before going into action.

She slipped into her dressing gown and made her careful way down the stairs to Hugh's study. She could withstand David's fury in the morning, but not the thought of Stephanie waking up, looking for Tatty Bear, and not finding him. Tatty Bear would be there, because she was going to fetch him from the study and tuck him in bed with Stephanie, so that she would see him the moment she opened her eyes.

She reached the study without mishap. She opened the door, and stopped. From under a pool of lamplight, David brought his dark head up from the paper he was reading.

'What are you doing here?' she gasped.

'Going over something that Hugh said he would like my opinion about. More to the point, what are you doing here? As if I didn't know!'

'If you know, why do you ask?' For once, her voice failed to reach the haughty note it achieved every time she found herself in a disadvantageous situation.

'You can come in, you know. I don't bite.' The shadow of a twinkle occupied the corner of his eye. 'I leave the biting to the bears, they do it so much better. The shaggy haired, carnivorous species that is, not the toy variety.'

'Where is he?' said Jan, trying to crush the smile bent on tugging up the corners of her mouth.

'Where is who?'

There was a plausible pause while Jan considered what may be behind his poker face. It savoured of something, but she wasn't experienced enough in the game of life to tell what.

She sighed, just a little wearily. 'Tatty Bear. Please may I have him to take up to Stephanie's room to tuck into bed with her so that she will see him first thing in the morning.'

'I cannot possibly concede to your request.'

With a nothing-to-lose desperation she let fly at him, with her fists beating against his chest, and an abuse of angry words to rattle his ears. 'You are the meanest, most impossible, most inhuman beast of a man I've ever met.'

He returned with hateful calm, and if the nonchalance was overdone she didn't notice, 'Everyone is entitled to their opinion. If you'll let me finish, the reason I can't hand that ridiculous toy bear over to you is because it isn't here.'

'Then . . . where is it?' But suddenly she knew the answer to that. Tatty Bear was in the very place she wanted him to be, and that was in Stephanie's bed. Moreover, she knew that David had put him there. And although she hadn't *seen* anything, she had caught him doing it.

The picture of him, as she had viewed him earlier in the evening when he'd come into Stephanie's bedroom just as she was leaving it, flashed vividly to mind. His awkward, hand-behind-his-back stance had been to accommodate Stephanie's beloved toy bear, and his mission had been to sneak it under the covers for Stephanie to find.

Jan hadn't thought it possible, but his voice went a crack icier. But that wasn't anywhere near as hard to bear as the sadness deepening in his eyes, and the hurt crinkling up his forehead as his words of reason flooded into her senses.

'If you'd used your head on thoughts instead of for blowing off steam, it would have occurred to you that I wouldn't dream of going out and leaving Stephanie without first returning her toy to her. Mrs. Miller might beat you hands down at child care, but she isn't you. This house may be far superior to the cottage, but it isn't home. Credit me with enough sense to know that a favourite toy compensates for a lot in a strange house.'

Later, Jan's better nature would take over, but just at that moment, as she cringed at the sadness of his gaze, it was superfluous consolation to know that Stephanie hadn't suffered the deprivation of her beloved bear while they'd been out.

He then said with unwonted gentleness, and although he spoke quietly the two little words bounced into her conscience like a shout: 'Goodnight, Jan.'

It wouldn't be. It would be an awful night.

CHAPTER FIVE

Thank goodness for those car radio cassette players. You click in the cassette and the car is filled with light music instead of heavy silence. Not that Stephanie was silent on the journey home, she chatted away non-stop above the music. At breakfast, in the presence of Linda and Hugh, David had appeared abnormally cheerful. Had he been putting on an act for their benefit? Did his moody silence now mean that he hadn't forgiven her for the mistaken, hot-headed, impulsive way she had attacked him yesterday?

As they got out of the car a cool little breeze blew round Larkspur Cottage, but the gate was open. The prosaic explanation was that it had been left open by an inattentive milkman or postman, but Jan preferred to look on it as a sign. It was open to welcome her back.

It was a cold lunch, and not merely because the ingredients for a ham salad had been taken from the fridge, but because of the atmosphere.

Depression is catching, and Jan thought it was as much her own as his that roused David to say: 'I'm sorry if I've been a bit quiet. Ralph, in his capacity as my solicitor rather than as a friend, said something to me before I set off for Hugh and Linda's that needed thinking about. I put it from me while I was there, but coming home has brought it back.'

Jan was highly relieved that he wasn't still annoyed with her, and slightly surprised at herself for thinking he might be. It wasn't in his nature to bear grudges. He was a strange man. Obdurate and unflinching. He'd won her hate first, then her heart. Could he now be winning her respect?

125

She took a thoughtful sip from her cup and said: 'This problem, is it something to do with the house transaction?'

'No. That couldn't have gone smoother.'

If it wasn't some hitch to do with the buying of the cottage next door, then what could it be? She dare not ask.

'Mrs. Weaver has moved herself out and the furniture and household goods she wants for her immediate use. The rest, mostly big stuff, is being collected by van and put into storage.'

'I'm sorry that I missed saying goodbye to Mrs. Weaver,' Jan said wistfully. 'I didn't know her all that well, because she was so rarely here. She seemed to spend most of her time visiting one or other of her vast horde of relatives, and when she was here she wasn't given to gossiping over the garden fence. But the little I saw of her was enough to know I liked her.'

'You will be pleased to know the feeling was mutual. Before she left she came round to say goodbye, and she said much the same about you. I got the impression that she was shy of pushing herself forward, but she wished she'd made the effort to get on friendlier terms. She entrusted me with a blue vase to give you as a keepsake.'

Jan hoped it wasn't the hideous blue vase she'd seen on Mrs. Weaver's mantelshelf the one and only time she'd entered her cottage. It was.

'It was a nice thought,' she said, oddly touched. 'You've got her address, of course? I must write and thank her.'

'Yes, somewhere. I'll sort it out for you. When you've finished your coffee, would you like to come and see what I've done with The Retreat?'

'The Retreat?'

'I can't keep calling it Mrs. Weaver's outbuilding, and it will be my retreat. Now that I've moved my bed in there, it will give you more room for your visitors.'

'If I have any. I haven't issued invitations.'

'I may have done on your behalf. I told your parents they'd be welcome any time.'

He was wearing a big 'Didn't I do well?' grin. She matched it.

'Thank you, David. That was most thoughtful of you.'

'Yes, wasn't it? It won't have done you any harm to strike out on your own, but until I met your father I didn't appreciate his feelings. Parental caring doesn't cease where independence begins. I like to think my impromptu visit sorted out any doubts yours may have been having.'

Jan was confident that it would have sorted out the existing doubts, but she thought it might have given rise to new ones.

She pulled a face at him for sounding pompous, kept her own surmises to herself, and was glad they were back on the old familiar footing.

Stephanie was playing in the sandpit. Taking a chance that she would be all right without supervision for a while longer, Jan said: 'Let's see what you've achieved, then.'

She knew that Mrs. Weaver had made alterations to the outbuilding to give extra accommodation to repay the hospitality of her large family, but she hadn't realised what a self-contained nest it made. It was divided into two main rooms, one for sleeping, the other for living in, and a separate room that was just big enough to take a washbasin and a shower unit. He'd taken some pieces of furniture from the house, the desk in particular looked good against the newly painted walls, but most of it he had been out and bought new. The deep, man-sized leather chair looked just the job for relaxing in at the end of the day.

'You've been busy with a paintbrush,' she said, and added with open admiration: 'How did you manage the curtains?'

'I cheated there. I wasn't up to tackling the sewing machine, so I went into Didsford and found a shop that made them up for me.'

'I call that using your ingenuity.' She remembered there was also a shop in Didsford, which was less than ten miles away and connected by a good bus service, that sold plaques with house names on them. She must make a point of going there and buying one with the name 'The Retreat' on it.

'You wouldn't like a nice blue vase, would you? It would look a treat on that table.'

'A treat I wouldn't dream of depriving you of.'

'It was a good try, anyway,' said Jan. 'You'll still be taking your meals at the cottage?' she enquired a little anxiously.

'Of course. You're not getting rid of me altogether. And I'd also appreciate it if you'd come in now and again and keep the place looking a bit something like.'

Now it was Jan's turn to say, 'Of course.'

'If you feel I'm putting on you, you can get a woman to come in and give you a hand.'

He must know he was not putting on her. When Annabel was alive she'd had her hands full, but the cottage itself was so easily run that nowadays she didn't have enough to do. When Stephanie resumed play-school (their visit to Linda and Hugh's had given her a short break) she thought she might fill her time by taking a bigger interest in the garden.

That evening, after supper, in the lull while drinking her coffee and before clearing away, Jan asked: 'You do think it's a good idea for Stephanie to keep on at play-school? Before—' Blast! She'd studiously avoided bringing Annabel into the conversation, but in this instance it was unavoidable. 'That is to say, when her mother was alive, more especially towards the end, I couldn't have coped with her all day. At the same time, it wasn't a case of farming her out. It was felt that the company of other children was good for her.'

'I agree wholeheartedly. Play-school is the best thing out for a child who hasn't got brothers and sisters to knock off the rough spots.'

Was he thinking that by now Stephanie should have had a brother or a sister, and regretting the circumstances that prevented it? Did he sometimes think that but for the car accident, Annabel, perfect in limb and vitally alive, might be sitting across from him now, laughter on her lips and love for him in her eyes? Poor, beautiful, tragic Annabel. Poor David. What should have been the happiest day of his life turned out to be the saddest when the car taking him and his bride from the church to the reception crashed. His best friend died outright, his bride was cruelly injured. It must have seemed like a bitter miracle when he stepped out of the wreckage unhurt.

And then—the facts were unarguable—David had left his bride-wife, and it could only be because he couldn't bear the thought of living with a cripple. Now that she knew him so much better she found it difficult to reconcile this callous act with the just, caring man she had found him to be. Perhaps the tragedy of it all had unhinged him for a little while. He must have loved Annabel deeply once. They had been everything to each other. Stephanie's existence proved that.

'I wonder what sad thoughts are behind that sad face,' David said suddenly.

She didn't reply. She couldn't.

His expression was ponderous. 'Tact isn't always the thoughtfully chosen word. Sometimes tact is saying nothing at all.'

His sapient words told her that he knew exactly where her thoughts had been. She didn't dissemble, but merely said: 'You are very astute, David.'

'And you are very curious.'

'They say a child endowed at birth with curiosity has been given a most useful gift. I suppose because curiosity is the source of all learning. I know it can also be a blight.'

'Poor Jan. Let's opt for a change of subject. You choose.'

'I was going to ask you about that French girl we saw last night,' she said brightly.

'Danielle?' He looked slightly taken aback.

'Yes. She left such a deep impression on me that I haven't been able to get her out of my mind. There's something . . .' 'haunting' she had been going to say, which wouldn't do at all. Remembering his version of tact, that sometimes tact is saying nothing at all, she improved on it slightly to meet her own use. On the lines that tact is the unsaid part of what you really think, she recovered in time to abbreviate it to, 'There's something about her. She called you and Linda and Hugh by first name. Is it because you're all old friends, or because you've been so often?'

'The one led to the other. At first I went, and presumably Linda and Hugh did too, because she was a friend and I wanted to give my support to her new venture. Now that she's established I go for the good food and entertainment. Danielle hasn't got much of a voice, but she makes the best of what she's got, and the same can be said of her looks.'

'There might be grounds for criticism about her voice, but you're being unfair about her looks.' Perhaps he didn't like petite, waif-like blondes. Remembering Annabel, a blue-eyed seductress with clouds of black hair, probably Danielle wouldn't be to his taste. 'I think Danielle has got an angelic beauty and a superb figure. I think something bad must have happened to her. There's a crying sadness behind her smile.'

'Couldn't that have been the style of song she was singing? Songstresses have to be actresses these days.'

'No. She's crying all the time inside.'

'You're right, of course. How observant of you.'

'I'm not being nosey. You don't have to tell me.'

'I think I do. I have to tell you because, on reflection, I think it would be a wise precaution, and not to satisfy your morbid curiosity.'

She supposed he had a point there. She did seem to have this knack of saying the wrong thing. But she felt, unhappily, as if she was prizing a confidence from him.

'Danielle was perfectly happy in her native country and had no thoughts of coming to England. But then she met an Englishman who was on holiday in France. Tall, dashing, a brilliant conversationalist, and apparently as knocked off his feet by Danielle as she was by him. She gave up her home and her family, and came to England with her fascinating Englishman. It was't all one-sided. In turn he gave her an engagement ring and introduced her to his widowed mother and his friends as his fiancée. It seemed all set for a fairy-tale ending, but then he died.'

Jan hadn't imagined it would be anything as bad as this. She thought of Danielle, so sweet, so breakably tiny, and she could have wept for her. What did she mean she *could* have wept? Her eyes felt suspiciously wet.

'How . . . awful.'

'It was bad for her. Danielle was the hardest hit of all of us.'

'Of all of *you*?'

'Poor Jan. You weren't to know. You didn't opt for a change of subject, after all. Danielle's Englishman was Stephen, the friend who died in the car crash that injured Annabel.'

Inadequacy is the torment of the soul, she thought, wishing she could take his proud hurt in her gentle hands, when all she was permitted to do was say, 'I'm sorry.'

'Don't distress yourself, Jan. It happened a long time ago now, and yet . . .'

She had an idea he hadn't meant to add that rider and finished it off for him. 'It's as vivid as yesterday.'

'Perhaps it is. But that isn't what I was going to say. I was going to say the repercussions are still having effect. I don't think it's ever going to let me go.'

She was biting hard on her lip.

He said: 'You can take that look off your face. It doesn't fit in with your role in life. Little girls are born to be protected, not to protect. Men are conditioned to turn their faces to the wall and get on with it alone.'

Did it have to be so? Did David have to stand so alone? Didn't he know that she was here? She knew he could never love her as he had loved Annabel, but if only he could accept her comfort she could love him enough for both of them.

She felt her chin being suddenly taken and tilted. 'Tears? I don't think anybody has ever cried for me before.'

Not for all the tea in China would she tell him that she wasn't crying for him. She was crying for pity of herself.

It wasn't until much later that she thought, something is wrong. It could be she wasn't in possession of all the facts, or if she was she'd constructed them wrongly in her mind. Something wasn't adding up.

*　　*　　*

David had gone back to work. Stephanie would have resumed play-school, but an outbreak of measles had closed it down for the time being. When Mrs. Grant, of Manor House, phoned to invite her and Stephanie to tea, Jan welcomed the diversion of this unexpected treat, and accepted readily.

While Annabel was alive, it had been the norm to take tea regularly at Manor House. Jan didn't know why, but it had been in her mind that this pleasant ritual would drop now that Annabel was no longer here.

Mrs. Grant had always sent a car for Annabel. Jan hadn't liked to ask if this V.I.P. treatment would be extended to her. She decided to wait on the off-chance of the car turning up, and if it didn't they would make up the time lost by taking the short-cut through the woods and round the back of the church.

Palmer, Mrs. Grant's chauffeur, perhaps anticipating Jan's dilemma, arrived early, and killed the waiting time with a can of beer in the kitchen of Larkspur Cottage.

The three of them, plus one very tatty toy bear which Jan would dearly have liked to leave at home, trooped out to the car.

'Little 'un's in a frisky mood,' Palmer

135

observed, his weathered face crinkling into a smile that told of his affection for Stephanie.

'You can say that again,' Jan said glumly. It was Stephanie's mischievous mood that had decided Jan to keep quiet on the subject of not bringing Tatty Bear. Hopefully, Stephanie would be too busy explaining to Tatty Bear exactly what was going on to get up to any high spirited jinks.

Palmer's easier manner relaxed her. As he drove carefully through the winding lanes, skirting the edge of the woods, he continued to be talkative and friendly, something he'd never been in Annabel's presence. He had always been very formal and correct with Annabel. He had awarded her the deference she demanded, but Jan had long ago formed the opinion that he had never really liked her. He was the only person she knew who hadn't been fascinated and charmed by the wit and beauty of Annabel.

'I hope you don't think it impertinent of me to ask, missy, but how is Mr. David going on these days?'

'He's keeping well, Palmer, but I don't think it's his health you're asking after, is it?'

'No, t'wouldn't be that, missy.'

'He's working very hard again, so I suppose that's a good sign. He's almost too busy to mourn.'

'I'm right glad to hear that. Mr. Stephen used to bring him to the house quite a lot. He

136

always had a friendly word for me. I right took to him.'

'So have I, Palmer. But we're in a minority group.'

'Reckon we are at that. They don't know what's what.'

'I don't either. I bet you could tell me, only you won't. And not because little pitchers have big ears.' Reference to Stephanie who was being unusually quiet.

'Reckon I don't have to. All the parts are there, like in a construction kit. It's only a matter of clicking them together. If you'll permit the liberty of my saying so, you're a bright girl. You'll figure it out for yourself afore so long.' Having stoked up her curiosity, he slammed in the damper against further questions by attracting Stephanie's attention. 'Did you see that squirrel, little missy? It ran right into the woods.'

'There are bears in the woods,' said Stephanie. 'Not Tatty Bears, great big growly bears. They go grrrrrrr . . .'

'I don't know about that. I do know there are badgers and deer and bats and owls. My little grandson plagued the life out of me to take him on a badger watch, until I finally gave in. We went at dusk to get settled like, afore the moon rose. Never again, I can tell you. We were frozen into balls of terror with all the strange carryings on, the moanings and the chitterings and the chatterings. T'were a right to-do. First it was the birds, the air was astir with all these black shapes pouring in their hundreds into the trees all around us. You should have heard the whirrings and the whistling and the piping and the whickerings. Sounds a daft thing to say, but the woods became alive with the sound of the birds and the animals settling down for the night. Didn't see no badgers, but we saw two small deer. Buck following a doe. Stepped as dainty as can be into the circle of the moon and just stood for a moment, absolutely motionless, like figures cut out of black paper. They got the sniff of us, I could tell by his twitching ears and her slender arching neck angling to peer into the dangerous shadows. Reckon he'd have stood the ground he was pawing with his forefoot, but she was uneasy like, and they disappeared in a flash, swallowed up by the undergrowth and the shivering darkness. And it wasn't only the darkness that shivered, I can tell you.'

Stephanie's eyes were round and entranced. 'Oh please, will you take me?'

'I wish I could, little missy,' he said, winking broadly at Jan, 'but my rheumatism has been playing me up something awful. You'll have to ask your daddy.'

Jan didn't think Stephanie would let it go at that, but she caught sight of the big black gates, and this effectively turned her attention.

Her nose flattened against the car window.

'Look, Tatty Bear, we're here. That's the fish pond which you haven't to fall into. And you mustn't push your sandwich down the side of the sofa because that's naughty, isn't it Jan? Jan, will there be cake with pink icing on it for tea?'

The symptoms of an 'interesting' afternoon were well in evidence.

Jan and Stephanie-and-Tatty-Bear got out of the car. Jan walked sedately towards the door, Stephanie and accomplice danced by her side. Out of the corner of her eye she watched Palmer drive the car away, either to garage it or turn it round ready for the homeward journey, with the distinct feeling of having lost a crutch.

Mrs. Palmer, Palmer's wife who was Mrs. Grant's housekeeper, opened the door to them. Her smile of welcome was as warm as Palmer's. By the time she'd chucked Stephanie under the chin and declared that she got prettier every day, Mrs. Grant was coming forward to greet them, looking every inch the gracious lady in a purple silk dress patterned with grey flowers, with pearls round her neck and dangling on fine gold wire from the lobes of her ears.

Neither her husband nor her son had been wise about money matters. Since their deaths certain financial disclosures had come to light which made it necessary for her to change her lifestyle quite drastically. She was a very proud old lady, adhering as best she could to the old standards and maintaining the dignity she felt her position called for, at the same time making no pretence to riches no longer in her possession. The paintings in the hall and throughout the house were copies. The originals had been periodically sold off to keep the place in a reasonable state of repair, but even that was beginning to prove a losing battle. A small army of servants had once been at her beck and call, but only the faithful Palmers remained.

'We are having tea in here,' Mrs. Grant said, throwing open a door and ushering her guests into a charming room with an Adam fireplace and sunshine falling in at the tall french windows. The kettle must have been on the boil because Mrs. Palmer followed them in almost directly. She put the tea pot and the hot water jug down on the table, and looked to Mrs. Grant for instructions.

'That's all right, Mrs. Palmer. Jan will pour, won't you dear? My hands aren't too steady these days,' she explained matter-of-factly, and not to seek sympathy.

'Of course,' said Jan, sitting forward. She turned her cup in her fingers, admiring the delicacy of the china and the tiny blue flower motif. 'What a beautiful tea service.'

'Yes, the forget-me-not was always my favourite.'

'Actually I'm a little apprehensive. Do you

think Stephanie should have a mug?'

'Thank you for your thoughtfulness, but no. I value people more than possessions. I've always used my things, and I'm too old to break the habit of a lifetime. When my mother-in-law died, her wedding present china was intact because it was never put to daily use. I thought it was so sad. I prefer my way, even with the risk of breakages. My dear husband used to tease me and say I'd change my mind when I had butter-fingered grandchildren to cope with, but I knew I wouldn't.' She looked at Stephanie with affection in the smile that curved her lips. It was impossible to see what her eyes were doing behind the tinted lenses of her spectacles, but the handkerchief pressed daintily to her nose was a clue. Was she thinking that had her son, Stephen, lived, she might well have been entertaining her own grandchild to tea instead of Stephanie?

She had lived most of her life in an atmosphere of opulence surrounded by treasures, but she had been denied the one treasure the poorest woman in the world may have in abundance: grandchildren. A woman like Mrs. Grant, who valued people more than possessions, would feel deprived indeed.

'I'm a sentimental old fool,' Mrs. Grant suddenly announced, blowing her nose and straightening her shoulders. 'I regret that little display. I don't often indulge myself and I'm

141

sorry if I've embarrassed you.'

'You haven't. I think I understand.'

'Do you, my dear?' The eyes behind the tinted lenses seemed to be looking at her with intense penetration. 'I very much doubt it.' Her mouth was firm, her manner so brisk that it was hard to believe that a few moments ago she had been overcome by emotion. 'Mrs. Palmer has baked all your special favourites, Stephanie, so I want you to tuck in. You too, Jan. I envy you your healthy appetite. I was always a little on the plump side myself and had to resist all the luscious fattening things. Now that it no longer matters whether I diet or not, I find that my appetite has gone. It's so unfair, don't you think?'

There was a brittleness behind her laugh and Jan suspected that her thoughts had gone back and she was dwelling on life's other injustices and deprivations.

Jan had been so engrossed with Mrs. Grant that she hadn't been watching Stephanie. Unsupervised, Stephanie had eaten the pink icing off four small round cakes, and if Jan didn't act swiftly a fifth cake, with its top bitten off, would join the other four.

'Stephanie!'

The smile she gave Jan was seraphic. She bit deeply into the cake in her hand and began to chew virtuously. Jan just had to smile.

But the smile was soon wiped off her face. It was the unexpectedness of it that was her undoing. She had been sitting in apprehension of something happening, but she had envisaged a piece of china getting broken. The plate very nearly was a casualty as Stephanie jumped to her feet. It fell to the floor, but thanks to a miracle, or the density of the carpet, it didn't break. Jan was down on her knees dealing with the spill of crumbs produced by all those uneaten cakes, when it happened. She heard Stephanie say: 'There now, we don't have to go into town for Tatty Bear to get some glasses.'

Jan stared in disbelief, horror and dismay. No! Stephanie couldn't have! But she had. She'd jumped up and before anybody could possibly know what was hatching in her mind, she'd snatched Mrs. Grant's spectacles from her nose and put them on Tatty Bear.

'Goodness!' Mrs. Grant blinked short-sightedly. 'Whatever made the child do that?' she added with such tolerance that it was Jan's turn to blink.

'I think I know. It's the result of a silly conversation Stephanie had with David ages ago. You think children forget, but they don't. It was all to do with the untidy state of her bedroom. Tatty Bear came into it, as he always does, and David said if Tatty Bear thought it was tidy then he needed glasses, and they'd better take him into town to get him fitted with a pair. Stephanie asked if he could have tinted ones like you wear and . . . oh, I'm so sorry.'

'That's all right,' assured Mrs. Grant, her mouth twitching in amusement. 'I don't suppose any harm has been done.'

It was the indignity Jan had been concerned with. She hadn't thought about anything more serious. 'I hope not,' she said earnestly, retrieving the spectacles from Tatty Bear and examining them for damage. 'They seem to be all right.'

In handing the spectacles back to their owner, and before they could be restored to their rightful place, she scrutinised Mrs. Grant's face for tell-tale signs of irritation, hardly daring to believe the genuineness of such a sweet and tolerant reaction. It was no fake. But even as she was thinking what an exceptionally nice person Mrs. Grant was, she was riveted by her eyes. They were her best feature. The tinted lenses had concealed not only the tranquil sweetness of expression, but the beauty of their colour. Such an exquisite peridot green. The same shade of green as Stephanie's.

Jan had often wondered whom Stephanie had inherited her unusual eye colouring from. Not from her mother, Annabel's eyes had been blue. Not from her father, David's eyes were brown. She had thought perhaps that Stephanie had a green-eyed grandmother, and she was devastated to think she might be right. But to be right about that, she had to be wrong about something else. If Louisa Grant was

Stephanie's true grandmother, then David couldn't be Stephanie's true father. Her father had to be . . . and she had even been called for him . . . Louisa Grant's son, Stephen. But Stephen had died in the car crash, and so by voluntary action, or because it had been forced on him, David had taken the role of father upon himself. *But David wasn't Stephanie's father.*

Jan tried to behave normally, as if she hadn't just made a most momentous discovery. But it was difficult to pick up the threads of the light-hearted chatter when her mind was reeling. On the other hand, Mrs. Grant had regained her composure and was talking away as happily as if nothing untoward had happened. As a child of her time, and station in life, the social arts and graces must have been part of her time-table, so it could be she was falling back on rigid practice. It also occurred to Jan that she could be at ease because she didn't know that Jan had suddenly hit upon this startling revelation. Why should she, now, after all this time? There must be those in Willowbridge who suspected, but they were obviously keeping quiet. Jan had never heard a whisper of gossip that might cast a doubt upon Stephanie's parentage.

Had David gone into the marriage knowing that the child on the way wasn't his? Jan didn't think so. Other things were beginning to make sense now. David wouldn't have deserted

Annabel because he couldn't face life with a crippled wife. But Jan could well believe that he would refuse to live with her if he found out he'd been duped. Annabel's pregnancy would have come to light when she was admitted to hospital after the car that was taking them to the reception met with an accident. Whatever she'd done, by that time she was David's wife, and he had honoured his responsibility to her, providing her and her child with a home and maintaining them both.

After all this time was the pain still there? What were David's thoughts when he looked at his . . . when he looked at Stephanie? It was going to take some getting used to the fact that Stephanie was not his daughter.

Jan let the tangled ends of her thoughts lay where they would, to be picked up and unravelled later, and made the effort to discharge her obligations to her hostess. Luckily, Mrs. Grant was in good form and the conversation flowed even though Jan's contribution was minimal. She could understand now why Mrs. Grant was tolerant towards Stephanie and why she made so much of her. When she looked at the child the love in her eyes took on a new meaning. When Stephanie trustingly put her hand in Mrs. Grant's as she walked them to the door when it was time to leave, a lump came into Jan's throat.

Some compulsion lifted Jan's chin and she

found herself reciprocating Mrs. Grant's keenly penetrating look.

'Please bring Stephanie again quite soon.'

'I will.'

Jan was sure that Mrs. Grant knew she was aware of her relationship with the child, but not a word was said.

Palmer opened the door for them to get in. Goodbye waves were exchanged, and they drove off.

*   *   *

'Reckon we're going to have a drop of our own,' Palmer said.

'Yes. I hadn't noticed, but it does look like rain.'

They could be in for a real downpour. Livid splashes of black rent the blue sky. By the time they arrived home there wasn't a speck of blue to be seen. The clouds met in floating black masses, squeezing out the last remnant of light, but despite one splash on Jan's nose, as they hurried from the car to the cottage, the rain held off.

Evening came. The air was hot and oppressive, but still it did not rain.

It was the usual drill for Jan to get Stephanie to bed and then dish up the evening meal, which she and David took together. She slowed down the simmering pans and returned to the living room with Stephanie's mug of cocoa.

'. . . please, Daddy, you've *got* to.' There was more mutiny than entreaty in Stephanie's eyes.

Whatever it was about—had David told Stephanie one bedtime story and was she demanding two?—David wasn't having any.

'No, young lady. It's way past your bedtime. Drink your cocoa and then it's up the wooden hill for you.'

'Tatty Bear doesn't like you,' she said fiercely.

'I'm sorry about that, because I like Tatty Bear. I love Tatty Bear,' he amended. And because he was talking in Stephanie-language, he meant 'I love you.'

He does, thought Jan, and that nuisance lump came to her throat again.

'Tell you what, if you're nippy about getting into bed, I'll come up and tell you a story.'

So Stephanie hadn't been pleading for a story. David never gave in. The promise of a story was used to distract her from whatever it was she'd been pestering him about.

Stephanie went upstairs with Jan, but it was under duress. As she tucked her in, Jan didn't much like the set of that mutinous little mouth.

David came down from telling that promised story just as Jan was putting the finishing touches to the table.

'Is she all right?'

'She will be.' He shook his head in

148

amazement. 'The ideas that pop into that child's head.' He didn't elaborate on that, but said: 'What sort of a day have you had?'

'A nice one, actually.' She wondered how he'd react when she told him where they'd been. She would have to tell him. If she'd known what the situation was beforehand, she wouldn't have gone without first asking his permission. 'Mrs. Grant phoned this morning and invited us to tea.'

If she hadn't been wised up she wouldn't have noticed the lift of his eyebrows, it was so slight. She saw because she was searching his face for some such reaction.

'You went, of course,' he said ever so casually.

'Yes. I didn't see any objection.'

'What objection could there be? I'm glad you had a nice time. Was Stephanie on her best behaviour?'

'Well,' she said wrinkling her nose, 'let's say second best behaviour.'

She didn't mention the incident concerning Tatty Bear and Mrs. Grant's spectacles, because it sounded too much like tale-bearing, and in any case it was too close for comfort to the revelation.

Although Jan had pointed out an interesting programme on television, when he'd finished his meal David returned to The Retreat. He'd brought some work home with him that he must do.

Having washed the dishes and finished straightening round, Jan went up to check on Stephanie. She popped her head round the door and gulped. There was something about the bed. It was too flat.

She flicked on the light and advanced into the room. She half expected Stephanie to jump out at her from the side of the dressing table or from behind the wardrobe. Nothing happened. Jan looked at the empty bed and went flying down the stairs and across to The Retreat.

She hammered on the door. David opened it to her, looking puzzled no doubt by the urgency of her knock, then concerned by the agitation on her face.

'Get your breath back. Then tell me slowly what's happened.'

'Stephanie's gone,' she gasped. 'I went up to her bedroom to see that she was all right, and she's not there.'

'Not there?' A look of disbelief crossed his face. 'Oh no! The little idiot.'

'You look as though you know where she's gone. Do you?'

'I'm not positive, but I think she's gone into the woods.'

'The woods. What for?' Jan questioned because her brain wasn't reasoning properly.

'To see the deer. She asked me if I'd take her and I said no because it was too late for her to be up.' So that's what Stephanie had been pestering David about. 'She must have decided to go by herself. I've no notion of how she got the idea of going on a deer watch.'

'I'm afraid I have. Palmer was telling her about the two deer he'd seen. She asked him to take her and he told her to ask—' Barely perceptible pause, because Palmer had said 'ask your daddy'—'you.'

'And I said no, so she's gone on her own.'

'Not quite on her own. She's got her accomplice in crime with her, dear old Tatty Bear.'

David was already pushing his arms into his anorak.

'Wait for me,' said Jan. 'I'll just put some shoes on.'

'You'll need your raincoat, and pick up a waterproof for Stephanie. The rain can't hold off much longer.'

It didn't. They weren't long out of the door and still not in sight of the black dense mass of the woods when the sky opened and the rain came down on them like driving spears. By the time they reached the woods, her toes felt waterlogged even though she was wearing sturdy walking shoes.

The overhanging branches slapped wetly against her face, the undergrowth put out feelers to trip her up. The light from the torch, which David had the foresight to bring, served the useful purpose of penetrating the path, but made everything look so much creepier.

'Poor little Stephanie. Wherever she is, she must be scared out of her mind.'

'Not Steph. She'll think she's having a huge adventure.'

'If she can think. If she hasn't fallen and knocked herself unconscious. She's so little. She could die of exposure.'

'Do you have a projector in your mind that switches on the horror stuff automatically? Instead of the H for horror, can we have a nice cosy U certificate?'

'You mean children's stuff, like Hansel and Gretel? Or what about *The Hobbit*. Tolkien can be relied upon for lifting a few hairs off the back of your neck.'

'Listen!' David commanded, silencing her.

She listened, but only heard the eerie moans and grunts and inhuman screams and screeches of the creatures of the forest. Perhaps it was the song they sang nightly, or perhaps they were objecting to the intrusion of two marauding strangers in their private little world.

'I was mistaken,' said David. 'Come on.'

They seemed to plunge on for ever, endlessly calling Stephanie's name. The trees banded together to take on weird shapes. Jan's imagination was working overtime and disembodied images were on the prowl in her mind. She told herself sternly that it was all in the mind, but kept an eye open for the odd spectral horse or headless huntsman.

She tripped and made a grab for David's hand. Even when she'd steadied her step, he did not deprive her of this comfort, and the warm cling of his fingers chased the ghosts away.

They found Stephanie hovering within the protective range of a large—and now oddly friendly—old tree. She was trembly lipped, but mutinous.

'I didn't see the deer. They didn't come and I waited and waited. And I was frightened that something nasty was going to get me.'

'In this friendly old wood?' Jan said, her voice squeaky with relief. 'There's nothing to be frightened of here. But you must promise never to go off on your own again. If we hadn't found you, you would have been very cold and wet and hungry by breakfast time.'

It was impossible to chide her seriously when all she wanted to do was hug and comfort her.

David was being very resolute and practical. 'If you do anything like this ever again, young lady, you can expect to be severely smacked.' He wrapped her in the waterproof he'd instructed Jan to bring along, but as it was a raincoat Stephanie was growing out of fast, it was hardly sufficient for the job. Without a word he took off his own anorak and snuggled her into it for added warmth, then lifted her into his arms and carried her all the way home.

Jan looked at the clock, expecting it to be

hours later. Impossible to believe, but slightly less than three quarters of an hour had elapsed between discovering that Stephanie was missing and now.

'Give her a warm bath, something hot to drink, and get her straight to bed. Do the same for yourself,' David instructed.

Jan's chin went up in a nod of agreement, and froze there. Before it had chance to come down again, Stephanie let out a scream that was more unnerving than anything she had heard in the woods, and would have sent a few of the woodland creatures scampering for safety.

The noise was still in her throat as Jan soothed: 'Everything's all right now, pet. You're home and safe, and soon you'll be snuggled up in bed.'

'Tatty Bear,' Stephanie sobbed bitterly. 'I left him under that tree.'

Two pairs of eyes looked at David, one waterlogged, the other expectant.

'No!' he said angrily. 'I'm drenched to the skin.' Having given Stephanie his anorak, that was no exaggeration. 'I will not turn out again to rescue a toy bear.'

Stephanie started sobbing and screaming again, more bitterly than before. Jan wrapped her arms round the heartbroken child, without letting her relentless gaze slip from David's face.

'You're being unreasonable, Jan. It's

154

inhuman of you to ask it of me. Stop that silly crying, Steph. I'll go in the morning and look. I'll buy you another bear, a bigger, nicer one.'

Stephanie kept on howling; Jan kept on looking.

'Damn the pair of you, no!'

'Then I'll go,' Jan said very quietly.

His eyes flew to the ceiling in exasperation. 'That blasted bear is the bane of my life. Women!' Shouting and spluttering he hauled his anorak back on over his wet shirt. He slammed out of the door, almost swinging it off its hinges, and shot off in the direction of the woods.

CHAPTER SIX

Things settled back to normal. Tatty Bear was awarded a medal for being such a brave little bear. He'd come out of his ordeal practically unscathed and only a little tattier than before.

Stephanie was back at play-school, quite happy to renew the acquaintance of her little friends after an intial bout of grumbling. David was more deeply immersed in his work than ever. He brought home masses of paperwork, and the light was often on in The Retreat until the small hours of the morning. David obviously got immense job satisfaction from what he was doing, but Jan worried that he might be overdoing it a bit. She shrank from mentioning this, because knowing David he would most likely tell her to mind her own business.

He was very guarded about what he considered to be his business. Without prying it was evident that the desk was kept locked and the key, which had always lived in the lock, was now missing. He had once accused her of riffling through papers that were no concern of hers. She had assured him that she hadn't, and was hurt by the significance of the missing key. Did he think the temptation to look might be too great, and that one day she would do more than lovingly caress the beautiful little desk with a soft duster? She never would have, even if she hadn't already discovered the desk's secret, that David was not Stephanie's father. Stephanie's birth certificate, which was presumably in the desk, wouldn't tell her anything. As Annabel's husband, surely David would automatically have been registered as Stephanie's father? But there might be letters or something else that gave relevant information.

Even though she was deeply grieved that David thought it necessary to keep the secret from her, she admired him for wanting to protect Stephanie. Perhaps he'd done it at first for love of Annabel. She knew now that when he came to Willowbridge after Annabel's death, the child had meant nothing to him and

156

was virtually a stranger. But the little stranger, with her mischievous and loving ways, had crept into his heart and now whatever he did was for Stephanie herself. She knew that if anyone tried to take Stephanie from him, he'd fight tooth and nail to keep her. Where had that thought come from? On paper David was officially her father. Nobody could take her from him.

She finished the dusting and let herself out. As she closed the door of The Retreat, it occurred to her that she hadn't followed up her intention of going into Didsford and buying a name plaque. Why not go now? She didn't have to collect Stephanie from play-school until this afternoon. And she could buy what she needed for the evening meal just as easily in Didsford. Easier, in fact, because there was a bigger selection of shops there than in Willowbridge.

She managed to catch the bus by the skin of her teeth. It was a soft and golden summer day, not the stifling heat of last week that had presaged that bad storm, and a playful little breeze lifted the ends of her hair and her spirits.

She decided that the plaque must be her first mission. The shop was at the bottom of the high street. She was just a little disappointed that it wasn't a wrap and carry service. She chose the shape of the plaque she wanted and the type of lettering from the

157

models on display, and had to be happy with the promise of an early delivery.

The requirements of a meal became her next priority. When the various packages were stored in her capacious shopper, the rest of the time available was her own, and she used it in pleasant window browsing.

She was looking thoughtfully at a richly patterned purple and black dress when a voice in her ear said: 'Not your style, *chérie*. You're not sultry and slinky.'

The attractively accented voice was unmistakable. Jan swung round with a smile on her lips to greet the petite French girl, the proprietress of Danielle's Den whose husky voice had entertained so charmingly, and who had left such a deep impression on her.

The hellos exchanged, Jan said: 'What is my style?'

'Something light and floaty and youthfully feminine.'

'Like me,' Jan said, wrinkling her nose in mild displeasure.

Danielle remonstrated gently: 'Not at all. I don't think you are light and floaty. I should say some down-to-earth thinking goes on in that head of yours. But I'm prepared to reserve judgement until I know you better. Do you have to dash, or can you spare the time for a coffee? There's a little café round the corner that is rather nice.'

'I've got an hour before my bus goes.'

'*Magnifique.* An hour is ample time to find out how David is getting on.'

They were settled in the café, with coffee in front of them, when Danielle said without preamble: 'And now I want you to tell me if David has got over all the terrible things that Annabel did to him.'

Nobody had ever before suggested that Annabel had ever done anything terrible to David. David was the one who had behaved abominably towards Annabel. David's godmother had said that he could have stopped the gossip. Her very words had been, 'With a name like his, you'd think he'd stone to death the Goliath of Local Opinion that's damning him.' Jan had replied that perhaps he hadn't the right stone. Linda had assured her that he had. But even Linda, who was presumably in knowledge of the facts, had never openly called Annabel.

'Have you lost your tongue, *chérie*, or is the question too difficult to answer? I know David is a complex man to understand, but surely it is apparent to you whether or not he is happy?'

'I haven't lost my tongue. My wits went astray for a while, but I'm in control now.'

'I'm afraid my derogatory remark about Annabel took you by surprise.'

'Yes. Nobody has ever breathed a bad word against Annabel. Everybody remembers her for her bravery, her beauty, and her sweet, uncomplaining nature.'

Now she came to think about it, she didn't know why Danielle's scathing opinion of Annabel should come as such a big surprise. Danielle was part of the tragic tangle. She had been engaged to Stephen, she must have been engaged to him at the same time as he was having an affair with Annabel. She might even know that Stephanie was Stephen's child and not David's. Her memory of Annabel would be bitter.

Danielle said: 'Who is everybody? If you mean the people of Willowbridge, they wouldn't know. It's doubtful if they'd set eyes on her before David installed her in the cottage.'

'Didn't Annabel come from Willowbridge? I thought she had.'

'No. It is traditional for the bride to be married in her home town. The village didn't become involved until . . . afterwards,' she finally produced in a flat, dead little voice.

Jan remembered that the tragedy which struck on Annabel's wedding day had claimed the life of Danielle's fiancé.

'Two people have very different memories of Annabel. David is one, I am the other.' A faint sigh escaped Danielle's lips. 'And even our memory of her differs. One of us will always see her as a monster, taking everything, giving nothing. Cruel, destructive, even from the grave. To the other she will always be a naughty child—thoughtless, but not intentionally cruel. A victim, perhaps, of her own incredible beauty.'

Danielle didn't say which version was hers. She didn't have to. Hers would be the bitter one. The less caustic version would be David's, because his memory of Annabel would be tempered by love.

Jan queried: 'I'll tell you what puzzles me. Why do you think David chose to house Annabel in Willowbridge? David didn't come from there himself. If he'd been one of their own they wouldn't have judged him so harshly. Why didn't David buy a house for Annabel in her own home town, where she would have been among people she knew?'

'I don't know. Annabel's parents died a long time ago and she was brought up by an indifferent aunt. That doesn't really answer your question. Whatever David's motive might have been, I'm sure it was a kindly one.'

That's what Jan surmised. In default of a positive answer, she could supply a pretty good guess. She thought David had chosen Willowbridge so that Annabel could be under the kindly eye of Stephen's mother. He hadn't forgotten Louisa Grant. She had suffered a cruel blow when she lost her only son. David was not going to add to her deprivation by not allowing her the joy of seeing her granddaughter grow up.

*   *   *

161

The day still had one more surprise for Jan tucked up its sleeve. She got off the bus at Willowbridge, and was walking along in a sort of thinking, dilatory fashion, when she saw two people whom she knew. She thought her mind must be playing tricks. It couldn't be them. She blinked and did a double-take and broke into an excited run.

'Why didn't you let me know you were coming?' And the next moment she was in her mother's arms and her father was in the process of relieving her of her shopping bag and dropping a kiss on her cheek. 'Darlings, I'm so happy to see you both. It's just too marvellous. You have come to stay? It's not just a flying visit?' she asked anxiously.

Her parents both answered at once. 'That's what I call a welcome,' her father said. Her mother's face was a beam of delight. 'We have. David gave us an open invitation and carte-blanche to take it whenever we wanted. And so here we are.'

Jan checked her watch. 'I don't have to collect Stephanie from play-school for an hour yet. There's time to go home and have a cup of tea.'

'You're talking my language. I'd love a cup of tea,' her mother said with feeling.

'Where have you parked the car?' Jan asked.

'Outside the cottage. When we saw that you

were out, we thought we'd have a little walk to stretch our legs and spy out the land. We were just sauntering along when we spotted you getting off the bus.'

On the way back to Larkspur Cottage, Jan walked between her parents, as she used to when she was a child, giving first one arm an excited squeeze, then the other.

Her mother thought the cottage was a gem in the perfect setting. 'It's the sort of sometime-in-the-future place we've always wanted. Oh, you are lucky to live here, Jan.'

Jan's shining eyes answered, 'Yes, I am lucky.'

She buttered some scones while the kettle was boiling and opened a packet of the ginger biscuits her father was partial to. The tea came very much secondary to the conversation, there was so much catching up to do.

Her mother followed her through to the kitchen and perched on the stool while Jan washed the few tea things up.

'Is it all working out for you, Jan?'

'Yes. I'm over Martin. That's what you meant, wasn't it?'

Her mother didn't look too sure that it was what she'd meant, but she nodded amiably.

'I never could keep anything from you, Mum, so I knew you must have guessed why I applied for the job in the first place. I thought I was heartbroken when Martin told me about Tara. I wasn't, of course. Broken hearts don't mend as easily as mine did. I had to get away because I couldn't bear the thought of seeing Martin and his new love together, as a team, the way we'd always been. But we'd never been a team in that way. Ours was a springtime love, young, fragile . . . a little foolish even. When I came home just recently, remember you and Dad were away when I landed? Well, I went out with Martin. The blossom had fallen from the bough and had drifted away. There was nothing but the sweetness of the memory left.'

'That's your impression, obviously. Does Martin feel the same way?'

'I don't know.' Jan frowned. 'I tried to get it across to him that it was all over between us, but I think I might have botched it.'

'I can tell you that you did. The message Martin got was that you were prepared to give him all the time he needed to get over the hurt Tara had inflicted, and that he could come seeking you out again, safe in the knowledge that you would be waiting for him with open arms. Which was rather conceited of him, I thought.'

It crossed Jan's mind that her mother had always tolerated Martin, without actually liking him.

'How do you know all this?' she asked.

'From Martin himself. He's been my most frequent visitor of late.' She pulled a face.

Jan's face wasn't exactly wreathed in smiles. 'I was hoping he would have made it up with

164

Tara by now.'

'If she's any sense, she'll think she's had a lucky escape,' Muriel Ashton said tartly. Then, 'What time did you say you had to collect Stephanie, dear?'

'Now!' Jan replied, pushing aside her mother's disquieting news and views to look at the clock.

*   *   *

Stephanie took to her parents like a duck to water. In turn, they were thoroughly enchanted by her. Stephanie took over completely. She jumped out of bed each morning as if she couldn't wait to unwrap this new day which represented a parcel tied up with promise and addressed to her. John Ashton was her devoted companion. It was his belief that a child's enquiring mind needed feeding, and he had the patience to carry it through. Her mother commandeered the kitchen and baked gingerbread men for her with currant eyes. As an extra bonus, David took time off from work and accompanied them on a sight-seeing tour of the surrounding district.

Jan had no idea who instigated it, perhaps her father did, but Stephanie dropped into the habit of calling him Gramps. Yet it never occurred to Jan how much like a family they looked until that lovely custom of taking after-

165

noon tea took them into a café with mullioned windows and a strategically positioned dessert trolley temptingly loaded with all manner of cakes and gateaus. The woman at the next table leaned forward and said to Jan: 'Your daughter is so sweet, but I bet she's quite a handful. How do you cope?'

Jan was so surprised that she hadn't the presence of mind to utter a denial.

To make matters worse the woman added: 'I've been trying to make up my mind who she takes after, you or your husband and I've decided that she's got a look of you both.'

Muriel and John Ashton had all on to suppress their giggles. It was left to David to jump into the breach. His reply was even more disconcerting than the woman's mistaken remarks. 'You should sympathise with me. They're both quite a handful. And I cope with extreme difficulty.'

'David, how can you say such an outrageous thing!' Jan gasped, her hand automatically lifting to her cheek, as if it might stem the flood of colour.

'My dear,' the woman said, misunderstanding totally. 'Don't be put out. I know from experience that husbands are the limit. You should hear the things mine says.'

All Jan could hear was her parents amused laughter; all she could see was the devilment sparkling in David's eyes.

Despite everything, it was a wonderful day.

Back at the cottage, Muriel Ashton said: 'Why don't you round if off by having a night out, Jan? I've told you before that you don't make the most of having a resident babysitter.'

'But it's your holiday, Mum. I'm content to sit with Stephanie while you and Father go out.'

'It's been a constant round of going out for me. I'm not used to it. At home, apart from my Whist-drive on a Wednesday and my Sequence Dance night, I rarely stir. While I've enjoyed the whirl, it will be nice to get off the roundabout for a few hours and put my feet up. You talk to her David.'

'Your mother's right, Jan. It will be a marvellous opportunity for you to have a night out.'

'But I don't want a night out,' she said, feeling a little annoyed that everyone was trying to manipulate her. 'In any case,' she said playing her trump card, 'I've no one to go out with.'

'I've thought about that one,' David said smoothly. 'Would you care to come out with me? We could have a meal somewhere.'

'I've got to prepare a meal for my mother and father,' she said stubbornly.

Muriel Ashton chipped in, addressing David first: 'I see she's still as argumentative as ever.' David's reply was a resigned lift of his eyebrows. Then she said to Jan: 'I am quite capable, you know. I've been married to your father for . . .' Jan found that she was holding her breath. When David had asked her age she had added four years to the twenty she could rightly claim. If her mother said she had been married to her father for twenty-three years, something wasn't going to add up. '. . . a considerable time.' Jan let her breath out slowly. 'And I haven't let him starve yet. Believe it or not, I have even had experience of putting a little girl to bed. So you can go out with David with a contended mind and leave Stephanie and your father to me.'

The one was not synonymous with the other. David's eyes met and held hers. There was a bright metallic twinkle in his that scratched her senses in some kind of electric warning. If she went out with David, contentment was the last thing she would know.

'Where would you like to go, Jan?' the man himself asked, taking the matter as settled. 'The choice is yours.'

'Danielle's Den,' she said decisively.

'Suits me. And this time I promise not to drag you on to the dance floor by brute force. You shall only dance if you want to.' As if realising that this teasing, flirtatious banter was being enjoyed by a third party, and Muriel Ashton was certainly looking on with a most intrigued expression on her face, he said: 'I promise it wasn't as bad as it sounds.'

'How disappointing!' was the prompt retort.

'Men, these days, underestimate the cave-man tactics.'

Fearful of what her mother might say next, and feeling that she knew what it was like to be ganged up against by someone in league with the devil, Jan made a hasty exit on the pretext of having to get ready.

*   *   *

This time Jan knew what to expect of Danielle's Den, but she still felt a prickle of excitement as she descended the stairs into the cellar-like atmosphere. The feeling of electric awareness could have had something to do with the tall man by her side whose hand securely clasped her elbow.

As they were shown to a table, Danielle, this time a slender sprite in midnight blue, waved to them from the piano, and changed songs practically in mid note. What mischief, Jan wondered, made her break into a song about a couple hovering on the brink of admitting their love? Her appealing, husky voice sang of the exquisite pain of love, the enchantment and misgivings of love.

It wasn't until David said: 'Does it have to be like that?' that Jan realised he'd been listening to the words as avidly as she had.

'In what way do you mean?' she asked, playing for time.

'Heights and depths. Surely one taste of the

169

bitter enchantment is enough? Next time round isn't it better to play safe and settle for a more temperate relationship rather than wait for a fever-pitch romance that might never happen again?'

Was he saying that he'd loved at fever pitch with Annabel, and rather than waiting around on the unlikely chance of this rare occurrence happening again, he was willing to put up with second best?

'I wouldn't know,' she said lamely. 'I'm not an authority on the subject.'

'I didn't think you were. But what about Martin?'

He couldn't possibly think that she and Martin had loved at fever pitch and that anything that came along for her now would be second best? No, no, it was too absurd. He must be referring to himself.

'What about Martin?'

'According to your friend, Sylvia, you applied for a job at Willowbridge to forget him.'

'I thought only women gossiped,' she said, stung that Sylvia had been so forthcoming. 'As I remember it, you didn't much care for it when I opened up about your private affairs.'

'No, I didn't. But I haven't been playing tit-for-tat. I didn't gossip about yours.'

'You're splitting hairs. You *listened*.'

'So I did. Are you hinting I should have shut her up?'

'It would have been the gentlemanly thing to do.'

'It never occurred to me.'

'Just as it never occurred to you to shut me up when I gossiped to you.'

'Are we arguing again, Jan?' he asked with a delicately speculative lift of one eyebrow.

'Of course not,' Jan said in a most argumentative voice, and immediately burst out laughing. 'We do tend to strike sparks off each other,' she admitted.

'I won't *argue* with that,' he said with amusing emphasis.

'Just when did you have this conversation with Sylvia about me?'

'You know when. That time I came to fetch you back from your parents'. I bumped into her on your doorstep, and as we were both at a loose end I took her out for a meal. I mentioned it to you at the time.'

'I thought you might have seen her since.' She wished she hadn't said that. It sounded as though she were jealous.

A point that did not slip by unnoticed. The evidence of this was apparent in the bright intelligence which came to his eye, a sharp twinkling force that had a pungent edge to it.

'Would you care to dance?' was the question his lips formed. His eyes conveyed a subtly different message, that was more in the nature of a challenge. 'Dare you dance with me?'

She had never seen him in this form before. It was nice, but it made her feel as though she was biting into ginger.

He was the best looking man in the place; come to that he was the best looking man she had ever seen, and he was looking at her in a way that gave her the shakes.

She walked on to the dance floor with a peculiar feeling of breathless excitement marking her apprehension. But the tightness of her breath was nothing to the hold David put on her. He held her closer than the shell is to the egg. She wasn't just dancing with him, she was melting into him. She wished she could get a grasp of the shakes. She liked to be in control of her own emotions, not bending vulnerably to his.

She knew what he was doing, but not why he was doing it. His half-slitted glance was appreciative of her womanliness as he lazily savoured her complaisance. It was as if he had sensed a responsiveness in her mood, and had worked on it to bring her to this thought-paralysing state of helplessness. As a husband he would often be impossible; but as a lover he would be perfect. He had the power to manipulate a woman; he would know exactly what to do to heighten her desire to their mutual delight and pleasure.

'I was right in what I said to that woman in the café, earlier today,' he said tenderly in her ear. 'You are a handful of woman. A

172

delectable handful. Is it improper of me to say this to you?'

'No,' she croaked.

'Then why are you blushing?'

'Am I?' she said. She could hardly tell him that she was blushing at her own thoughts. At the intimacies her mind had conjured up in disquieting detail.

She saw the look in his eyes—smile or triumphant gleam?—she wasn't sure which but she could make a pretty good guess. And she knew to her deepening dismay that she couldn't even claim these thoughts as her own. To the last intimate detail, he had projected them into her head.

She objected to the idea of being this malleable in any man's hands. It was tantamount to giving herself to him to do with as he pleased without a qualifying clause. If the man loved her enough, that would justify her susceptibility, because he would put her first. The right kind of love would be a giving love, not a taking love. It would protect, not hurt. Warm, not consume.

But . . . she was getting confused . . . love? Love is a tender flame. Shared mistrust cannot ignite it, and it doesn't flare into wild antagonism at every turn and twist of thought. Undeniably there was something between them, and she had always known that it would taunt just so far before reaching a point from which there was no drawing back. Whatever it was on his part, on her part it was love. She could never honour truth again if she didn't own up to that. Her physical urges were a strong match to his, but she knew that in her it was an impulse that came straight from the heart. She was a woman and so her heart had to be touched before her senses were alerted. He was a man, and men aren't quite so fastidious.

The music ended. They walked back to their table and resumed their places in silence. It was probably silly of her to harbour the comforting notion that he seemed to be as shaken as she was.

'Well,' he said, picking her hand off the table and holding it.

Her heart contracted at the look in his eyes. A look like that must surely come straight from his heart. Nobody, not even David, was skilful enough to manufacture it from the senses.

He turned her hand over and placed his on top of it so that they lay palm to palm. His longer fingers caressed the sensitive area on the inside of her wrist. She was frightened, not of him but of herself, and alarmed that his touch could pinpoint so much feeling in her.

'It's all wrong, Jan. I shouldn't say a word to you before I've explained everything to you. It's putting the cart before the horse.'

She couldn't condemn him for that. She'd always had the unfortunate knack of putting things in reverse order herself, and she had made no exception when it came to her feelings for him. Because of what gossip said, she hated him before she knew him. Because of some strange power he wielded over her, she loved him before she liked him.

'Sooner or later you are going to marry me. It would make it easier for me if it were sooner.'

'Hasn't anybody ever told you that a man should honour a girl with a tender, questing proposal?' she said, choking over the unexpectedness and abruptness of it.

'Hasn't anybody ever told you that a man regards marriage as a bitter confiscation of his freedom? The fact that I'm prepared to give mine up should be enough.'

He was like a little boy, she thought. Touchingly unsure, brusquely hesitant, for all his tough words.

'I don't know what to say.'

'Yes will do.'

'Yes.'

'There. That wasn't very difficult, was it?'

She laughed joyously, shook her head disbelievingly. She thought that if David didn't take her out of here quickly she would exhibit a complete lack of control and rush round the table and into his arms.

It was deflating, shattering, to see David abandon her hand for his knife and fork and calmly begin to eat the meal she couldn't remember being ordered, never mind being set before them.

He made her feel warm again by saying: 'How quickly can you eat? If we got up to go out leaving our food untouched, Danielle would beat us to the door to ask why.' His eyes flicked across to the piano. 'I'm afraid she's coming over in any case. Probably to ask what we find more interesting than the food we have delayed eating for too long. All will be forgiven when I tell her.'

For some inexplicable reason, Jan didn't want Danielle to be told, not just yet. She wanted to keep it safe and secret. David had put the cart before the horse. He'd proposed without doing the courting and the cosseting. Until he'd done the courting and the cosseting she wouldn't feel properly engaged; she wouldn't feel safe. She knew she was being trivial and unreasonable, and to make up she gave David a lovely smile of reassurance.

And, anyway, Danielle was a woman, and there are some things a woman doesn't have to be told, at least not in so many words. The shining radiance in Jan's eyes was blazoning the news to the world.

'Jan had just consented to be my wife,' David said, sounding smug and pompous.

'I'm so pleased,' Danielle bubbled with absolute sincerity. 'It will make it easier for you, David.'

Jan frowned. David had used much the

same wording. 'Sooner or later you are going to marry me.' And then he had said: 'It would make it easier for me if it were sooner.' What she had taken to be his meaning had put a blush to her cheeks. But Danielle couldn't mean the same thing.

Danielle said: 'I must sit down before I fall down. And I had you marked as a person of high intelligence, Jan. How can you take on this bitter old cynic?'

Unperturbed by Danielle's seemingly unfavourable opinion of him, knowing she was only teasing, David snapped his fingers to alert a waiter. 'Bring another glass, please. You'll take a drink with us, Danielle?'

'Yes, but not this,' she said, delicately wrinkling her nose at the wine on the table and tapping the bottle with a shimmering blue-pink fingernail.

'According to your wine waiter, it's the best in the house. And at the price you charge for it, it should be,' David said, quirking an amused eyebrow at her.

'Oh, it is. There's nothing wrong with the wine. It is of an excellent year, but it is not appropriate for the occasion. Bring champagne,' she said to the waiter. 'The best we have. Only the finest champagne is good enough to toast your happiness. I'm truly delighted for you both. He's quite a nice bitter old cynic once you get used to him, as you must know, Jan.' She leaned forward and touched David's arm. There were tears in her eyes as she said: 'We have both known a bad time. Yours is now behind you. Let it be that way, my friend, by remembering only what was good. Don't let yesterday's bitterness spoil your beautiful tomorrow.'

She went on to say something about it being in bad taste to stir up unhappy memories, but she was doing it in David and Jan's best interest. 'It is necessary to your happiness to forgive, David,' she beseeched.

Jan's mind harked back to the conversation she'd had with Danielle in that café in Didsford. Danielle had recalled memories of Annabel from two viewpoints, hers and David's. They both remembered Annabel in a different way. To one of them she was a monster, taking everything, giving nothing; cruel, destructive, even from the grave. The other saw her as a naughty child—thoughtless, but not intentionally cruel, a victim of her own incredible beauty. Annabel had borne a child by Danielle's fiancé, and Jan had naturally thought that hers would be the harsher memory, and that David's would be tempered by love and therefore he would have kinder thoughts of Annabel. But Danielle was saying that it was David who harboured the bitter memory and until he let it go he would not be able to find true happiness.

'You haven't a drop of bitterness or resentment in you, have you Danielle?' David said.

'Why should I have? I shall always be grateful for the happiness Stephen gave me. Now that he's dead, I want him to rest at peace. I have no quarrel with the living. The only person I would hurt by keeping my vengeance alive would be myself. Would it right the wrong if I vented my anger on a child who didn't ask to be born? No blame can be attached to Stephanie. She must not suffer for the mess we made of things.'

So Danielle knew about Stephanie. Somehow this did not surprise Jan.

'Ah! Here is the champagne,' Danielle said. The moment hers was poured she lifted her glass, but did not touch it to her lips. 'To you both. Champagne is such a happy drink. It laughs and bubbles in the glass.'

Let our life together be like that, Jan thought. David had suffered pain and humiliation. From this moment let it be laughter and happiness. With the plea, a gentle little sigh seemed to ease itself round her heart. She had no warning that her relief was premature. She thought what a beautiful person Danielle was, beautiful inside as well as outside. She was so happy for them. Chattering away, planning.

'You'll have to get married quickly, you know, to make it right with the authorities. The promise of a marriage won't be enough, and I'm sure that you, Jan, won't mind

179

forgoing the sort of massive wedding that takes ages to arrange, when a quickie job will tie the knot just as securely and at the same time ensure that everything goes smoothly with Stephanie's adoption. I can, and do, sympathise with Mrs. Grant, but it's wrong of her to deny Stephanie the right to grow up in a young household. After all, you have never denied her the opportunity of seeing Stephanie. And it isn't as if Stephanie would benefit financially from belonging to Mrs. Grant because the money has all gone and she is living in pathetically reduced . . .' Her exuberance faded as she saw, too late, David's frown and Jan's dismay. 'What is it? Oh, David, don't tell me you haven't told her?'

'No, I'm afraid not. I hadn't got round to it yet.'

'But you should have done. Oh, *David.* I am so sorry. I did not mean to be indiscreet. I assumed, because you'd proposed, that you would have told Jan *everything.* What can I say?'

'Nothing more, please,' David said in a quiet voice. 'Just go. Don't worry,' he added in a kinder tone. 'No harm has been done.'

'I hope not,' Danielle said, her eyes trailing unhappily from David to Jan. 'I will see you later, *chérie.*'

As soon as Danielle went, Jan said: 'I don't understand this talk about the authorities. What did Danielle mean?'

'I will explain,' he said tersely, 'but not here. I think the evening has just folded up on us. I'll take you home, and explain it all to you there.'

'Very well,' said Jan, rising with dignity and walking away from the table where the untouched champagne continued to sparkle and bubble in the glasses, but now the atmosphere was more consistent with the ice in the bucket. Her fault, she knew. David looked irritated and annoyed, but he wasn't cold towards her, although he didn't offer to take her hand as they walked to the car.

Conversation was sparse on the journey home, again her fault. Her mind was numb to everything but the strange wording of David's proposal. 'Sooner or later you are going to marry me. It would make it easier for me if it were sooner.' She had thought his stilted brusqueness had stemmed from shyness. But when he told Danielle she had said, 'It will make it easier for you, David.' She wanted him to marry her because he loved her, not to make it easier for him, whatever that could mean. It was something to do with Stephanie, obviously.

She had already guessed that David was not Stephanie's true father. She thought that when he came to Willowbridge after Annabel's death he had been kind to Stephanie out of compassion, but in a miraculously short time he had come to love her as his own. Danielle had mentioned Mrs. Grant. Was she some threat to David's chances of being allowed to keep Stephanie? Had Mrs. Grant decided to come out in the open and publicly claim Stephanie as her grandchild? Danielle had also said something about adoption. Was David negotiating to adopt Stephanie? But if so, why? As Annabel's husband, David would automatically have been registered as Stephanie's father. She wasn't well up in these matters, but surely by the law of the land, on paper at least, David was Stephanie's father.

On parking the car, David nodded his head towards The Retreat. 'Do you mind stepping into my den for a moment? I see the light is out in the cottage, which means your parents are in bed. I'd prefer not to run the risk of one of them coming down for something. I want to say what I have to without fear of interruption.'

Jan conceded with a cold little nod. David looked grim about the mouth as he inserted the key in the lock and pushed the door open for her to enter.

Her cool manner had got through to him, and as she made to pass him he gripped her arm and said with a flash of anger: 'It would have been better if I'd got in first before you got a garbled half-account from Danielle. But I don't know what you are getting uptight about. You knew there were things I had to tell you.'

There was a well of tears behind her eyes

that at all costs must be suppressed. Her chin lifted spiritedly. 'How could I know?'

'Because I told you. When I proposed I said that I was putting the cart before the horse.'

'Strange as it may seem, I thought you meant you should have courted and cosseted me first and then proposed.'

The flashing sparks did not leave his eyes, but were joined by a look of compunction. 'Of course,' he said, and he sounded just a tiny bit incredulous.

He mustn't be allowed to go tender on her. She couldn't bear that. Such things shouldn't be prompted.

She walked away from him. He didn't try to hold her. She walked over to the Sheraton desk, stroking a finger across its smooth surface. 'I never looked, you know. I'm not the prying sort. But if I had, what would I have found?'

'It's not exactly what you would have found in there. It's more what you wouldn't have found.'

'I don't understand.'

'If you'd looked among all the important documents, you would have spotted one omission. You wouldn't have found a marriage certificate. I wasn't married to Annabel.'

CHAPTER SEVEN

'The wedding never took place,' David said. All emotion was expunged from his voice. His face, quite devoid of expression, was held in such rigid control that Jan thought something must crack.

And still she couldn't take it in.

'But Stephanie carries your name,' she protested. 'Annabel introduced herself to me as Mrs. David Spedding.'

'Anybody can be known by any name they choose.'

'She told me that she was married to you.'

She was battering him down with futile dissension. She knew she must let him tell it in his own way, but it was difficult to keep her mouth buttoned up. Especially when he said: 'She told everybody that. I didn't refute it.'

Why? her mind screamed, but she kept her mouth closed.

'The preparations for the wedding were made—' He allowed himself a slight grimace here—'Such as they were. Annabel wanted a quiet wedding, she said. Surprising, really, because she was such a flamboyant person. Being the type who does not like a lot of fuss, I was too relieved to question her choice, or look for a hidden motive. As far as she was concerned, it turned out to be one of her better decisions. Nobody paid overmuch attention to the fact that a quiet wedding had not taken place. Annabel herself must have propagated the lie that the car she and Stephen were travelling in crashed on the way from the church to the reception, and that I was in the car with them. Who would have thought there was an old-fashioned streak in her that, because of the coming child, would make her want to appear married? It didn't strike anybody as odd that I walked out of an accident, without a mark on me, that left one person badly injured and proved fatal for the other. I was never in the car, of course. But I wonder what they thought?' His eyes on Jan were keen and penetrating. 'That the devil looked after his own, perhaps?'

It was too near her own thoughts for Jan not to blush as she stammered: 'So you're not a widower?'

'No, I'm not. When you marry me it will say bachelor of this parish on the marriage certificate, or whatever the wording is.'

Ignoring his presumption that she was still going to marry him, Jan said: 'If she wasn't your wife, why did you make yourself financially responsible for Annabel and . . . Stephanie?

The pause before saying Stephanie's name was too significant to be missed.

His eyes narrowed. 'Just because I wasn't married to Annabel does it automatically follow that Stephanie couldn't be my child?'

'Of course it doesn't,' Jan said gruffly. 'I only know that she isn't. You're not Stephanie's father.'

'Perhaps you know who her father was?'

It was revealing that he said was and not is, and confirmed her suspicions.

'Yes. It was Stephen.'

'Would you care to tell me how you know?'

'Because of the family likeness. Oh, I never met Stephen, of course. I mean the likeness to Stephen's mother, Mrs. Grant. Stephanie's got her eyes. And it accounts for her interest in Stephanie. She must know that she's her granddaughter?'

'Yes.'

'Did you . . . ?' She bit hard on her lip, sealing in the question.

'Ask me. It's natural for you to be curious.'

It was unnatural of him to be willing to feed her curiosity. She hesitated, then plunged. 'I was going to ask if you knew that Annabel was having an affair with Stephen?'

'I'll answer that gingerly. I didn't know it had gone as far with them as it had. I was intoxicated with Annabel, can you understand that? To give him his due, so was Stephen. But he had a better head for such things. We met Annabel through my godmother. As I remember it, Stephen and I were dragged, much against our will, to one of those parties to launch a new beauty product. Annabel was

186

there because she did a bit of modelling for Linda's firm.'

'Was she a model? She never said what type of work she did before, but I had wondered if it was something to do with fashion or beauty. Even as she was, she retained her poise, and she was very beautiful.'

'Yes, her training stood her in good stead. She was beautiful, and we were bored. The party wasn't our line of thing at all. It was inevitable that we both made a play for her, and then found her exciting enough to want to continue seeing her afterwards. The sense of rivalry made both of us that much keener.'

'I'm trying to fit the time thing in. Where was Danielle while all this was going on?'

'Around. Stephen was engaged to Danielle,' David answered explicitly. 'He had no intention of giving her up. Yet he wouldn't let the little matter of a fiancée spoil his fun. The field was by no means clear for me. In fact, if my ego hadn't had blinkers on, I would have known he was the hot favourite. When Annabel turned my first two marriage proposals down, I wasn't unduly put out because I thought it was traditional. When she said yes at third try, I thought it was because she'd teased me long enough, and not because she'd come unstuck with Stephen.'

This was one of the things Jan had never been able to understand. Too-loving, naïve little girls might still get themselves into this sort of scrape, but not someone with Annabel's high sense of self-preservation. No, it hadn't 'just happened' to Annabel. She was born with ancient wisdom.

David continued where her thoughts left off. 'I'm inclined to believe that the baby was a deliberate slip. She was too cute to have been caught out. When it came down to it she wasn't as wise as she thought. He refused to break with Danielle to marry her. And so she decided to settle for me, a nice, handy scapegoat.'

'But you found out, and called the wedding off?'

'No, I didn't find out. Not until afterwards. I didn't call the wedding off. I was on the point of setting out for the church, when word was brought to me of the accident. You're wondering what Annabel was doing in a car at that time with Stephen?'

She wasn't. She'd assumed that Annabel had decided not to hire a taxi for the purpose and that Stephen was driving her to the church. It was a bizarre thought, but then the situation didn't exactly conform to convention.

'She didn't believe that Stephen would let her go through with it. Up to the last moment she hoped Stephen would change his mind. It was always Stephen, never me. She used me to bring him up to scratch.'

'You can't know that for sure,' Jan said, hating to see this proud man's ego so cruelly crushed. She could have saved her breath.

He replied grimly: 'I can. Annabel told me. She was in the car with Stephen when it crashed, because she was making a last desperate bid to bring him round to her way of thinking. They started to row, and in the heat of the moment Stephen lost vital moments of concentration and the car slammed into a brick wall. I believed her because it was the only way it could have happened. Stephen was a very competent driver.'

'I'm so very sorry, David. Sorry for misjudging you,' she added hastily in case he thought she was giving him pity which he would hate. 'I . . . like everybody else . . . thought you'd deserted Annabel, whereas you settled her in a house, supported her and allowed her to take your name even though she had no right to it.'

'I had my reasons. But I'd question that they are the praiseworthy ones you are crediting me with. We once had a discussion on the subject of pride, do you remember?'

'Yes. How Annabel's pride must be upheld.'

'Sometimes, when I'm in a benevolent mood, I like to think I did not correct the lie of our marriage to keep Annabel's pride intact. But when I'm in an honest mood, I know it was to preserve my own. It's not a very pleasant admission to make, but I took on the responsibility of Annabel and her child so that people wouldn't know what a fool I'd been.'

'Oh?' Jan queried gently. 'And is it pride that makes you want to hold on to Stephanie now, because if you let Mrs. Grant have her everybody would know?'

'What other reason could I possibly have?'

'You've grown fond of Stephanie, you know you can do better for her than Mrs. Grant can. David, you're a fraud. Admit it to yourself, even if you won't admit it to me. It wasn't pride that sent you back out in the driving rain to retrieve her disreputable toy bear from the woods when you had stated categorically that you wouldn't go.'

'I backed down on one occasion. Every man is allowed one moment of weakness.'

'One moment? Just one occasion? It wasn't pride that made you humble yourself sufficiently to sneak the bear up to Stephanie while we were staying with Linda, after you'd put him in solitary for breaking Linda's cold frame. That wasn't pride. That was kindness and caring and compassion.'

In that moment of loving him more than she'd ever thought it possible to love anybody, she knew she couldn't marry him. It had to be the heights and depths, or nothing at all. She knew that it could never be the same for him as it had been with Annabel. He wouldn't want it to be. Why couldn't the difference be for the better? The same bitter-sweet, fever-pitch enchantment, but a different girl adding the extra piquancy.

190

She knew she couldn't be his second best. It would be heartbreak and humiliation to love him this much, and not occupy first place in his heart. She was shocked by the power and depth of her feelings for him. He had liberated the woman locked in the little girl. To look at him was to want him. She dare not meet his eye in case he saw the invitation in hers. She dare not allow him to touch her because she knew that if she did there would be no holding back and she would give herself to him completely.

Woman's primeval urge in a difficult situation is to run. That's what she must do. She must get right away from him. More urgently now, at this moment, she must go before she weakened and did something silly. And then tomorrow she must make plans to effect a complete break. When her parents left, she would go with them.

But what about Stephanie? It was a question without weight to it. Her heart was looking for an excuse to stay. Her mind was hammering it home that with David around, Stephanie was in the best possible hands. The strongest hands. He would fight a dozen Mrs. Grants; he would climb every rung of the law, propping the ladder at the highest level of the country to keep Stephanie. The most sensible hands. He would be firm, but just. He would discipline with tolerance and commonsense, and his judgement would be tempered with warmth and humour. The most loving hands. Dare Jan dwell on the gentle love he would have for a child? Or the passionate love he would have for a woman? He would know when a woman desired to be swept into submission by force, and when she needed to be pampered with patience and given lots of time and endless reassurance. He would always be tender.

He made a movement, a sort of scuffing noise on the carpet with his foot, and she was terrified that he was going to come over to her. Her throat was tight and hot with emotion, and her hands were as shaky as her voice.

'It's terribly late. I should go.'

'I don't want you to, but I must agree with you. There's tomorrow . . .' She could hear the smile, the lazy indulgence in his voice. 'I'll tell your parents,' he said on a deeper, authoritative tone. 'Your father first. It will be a nice touch to ask for permission to marry his daughter.'

'No,' she croaked. 'I . . . I'm sorry, but I can't m-marry you.'

'The traditional turn-down, Jan?' There was surprise in his voice.

And reproach in hers as she said: 'You know that's not my style. I can't marry you, and now I'm going. And that's the end of it.'

'I won't detain you,' he said. True to his word he didn't put out a staying hand as she crossed to the door and opened it. 'But that's not the end of it,' he added ominously.

* * *

Jan slept badly, tossing and turning and finally waking up in a panic to see that it was nine-thirty. She was surprised that Stephanie, who should have been taken to play-school half an hour ago, hadn't bounced in, demanding that she wake up. She scurried into the bathroom, washed and dressed, and paid scant attention to the pale little face in the mirror above the wash-basin.

Downstairs, only her father was there to witness her hurried descent.

'Where is everybody?' she asked.

'David's gone to work. Your mother's taken Stephanie to that school effort of hers, and on her way back she's calling in at the newsagent's because the paper boy has missed us again.'

Jan smiled tolerantly. 'He's not good at getting up in the mornings, either. He constantly runs the risk of being late for school, and with Larkspur Cottage being at the very end of the village . . .' She left it there. 'I take it everybody has had breakfast?'

'Except you.'

'I'll skip it this morning. I'm not hungry.'

'You look peaky,' her father said critically. 'Is something bothering you?'

Jan's eyes, the famous Ashton eyes, lightened to green good humour as she said with a deprecating shake of the equally famous Ashton rich chestnut hair: 'Never could keep anything from you, Dad. I want to come home with you when you go.'

'For a holiday?'

'For good.'

'What does David say?'

'I haven't told him yet.'

Her father gave her a sage look. 'This wouldn't be an emotional decision, would it, Jan?'

'I don't know. I only know it's the right decision for me.'

'For you, Jan? That's not your usual slant of things. What about Stephanie?'

'Stephanie will be all right. She's got David.' She had no idea what a very revealing thing she had said.

Had she looked at her father she would have seen the relaxing of his expression as he replied: 'So have you.'

'What?'

'Got David . . . to deal with, that is.'

'Oh . . . yes.'

'Can you manage? Or do you want a bit of fatherly weight behind you?'

'Would you give me it if I said yes?' She permitted herself a small mischievous smile. 'Or would you say what you did that time when I was a little girl and came in crying because the big girls had taken my doll and pram from me.'

'It doesn't seem all that long ago at that,' he said nostalgically, 'but perhaps you can refresh my memory. What did I say?'

'You told me I was big enough to stand-up for myself and you made me go back and face them. You said shirking problems was a bad habit to get into and I may as well start as you intended me to carry on.'

'Did I? What a wise father you've got.'

'Yes I have. Oh, I do love you.'

'I love you. We're lucky, you know, in our family, that we can say that so easily. Three little words. I love you. They roll off the tongue. Yet some people don't find it an easy thing to say at all. Some people find it most difficult. I suppose it's a family thing, whether they say it, or express it in other ways. Yes, we're lucky in our family. All it needs to know you're loved is a reasonable pair of ears, not an astute piece of detective work.'

'What are you going on about?'

'You are quite right. I am rattling a bit, aren't I? Ah! Here is your mother.'

His face lit up in a smile, as it always did when she came into the room he was in. It was a reciprocal thing. It was nice to have parents who, after twenty-three years of marriage, could still light up for each other. But Jan thought there was also a flicker of relief on her father's bright face, as if on this occasion he was glad to see her mother because it put an end to his conversation with her.

Her mother announced that she would like to go to Harrogate for the day. When her father asked if it was for the purpose of leisurely browsing or serious shopping, the prompt reply was that he should take his cheque book with him.

Jan was surprised not to be asked to go with them, and in a way she was glad. She wanted to give the cottage a thorough going over so that it would be in tip-top order when she left. While her parents were out of the way it would give her the opportunity she had been looking for.

She had finished washing down the doors and was concentrating on the skirting board and window-sills, when the phone rang.

It was Martin on the line, sounding very sorry for himself indeed.

'I'm in desperate need of cheering up. I thought around, and of all my friends I selected you, sweet, kind, sympathetic Jan, as being the most qualified for the job.'

'Oh dear, I do hope I justify your faith in me. I'm not in a very cheering-somebody-up mood. What's the trouble?'

'I've done something so silly, it's unbelievable. I thought I was getting a tiny bit too paunchy, and so I enrolled at one of those health clinics. You know, squash, saunas, that sort of thing. Anyway, they gave me a list of exercises to do. All highly tested and very commendable, only I started to do them without first taking the precaution of removing my dressing-gown. Wouldn't you know, I tripped over the damned cord, put myself out and ended up in the casualty ward of the hospital and now my arm is in a pot.'

'Oh, Martin, you idiot!'

'Do you mind! I feel bashed about as it is without being called names. If you're going to be like that, I'll ring off.' He sounded petulant.

'No, don't do that. Are you working?' An idea was beginning to buzz round in her mind.

'Not a chance. It's my right arm. I'm practically immobilised.'

'In that case—' She took a deep breath— 'Why don't you come up here for a few days and be pampered?'

'That is the most tempting offer I've had so far. But . . . I don't see how I can drive my car with a broken arm,' he said plaintively.

'Have you never heard of public transport? There's a perfectly good rail service that will drop you off within a stone's throw of here.'

'But, sweetie, trains are so tedious.'

'Oh well, if you don't want to come.'

'Did I say that?'

'It would only be a one-way strain because my parents are here and you'll be able to get a lift back with them.'

'And here I was thinking you were out to compromise me. I shall swallow my disappointment and see you some time this evening.'

As Jan set the phone to rest, smiling a little at Martin's audacity, she felt that she had taken a step in the right direction. She wasn't quite sure what she had in mind, but she felt that in some way Martin's presence would make it easier to resist David. She had never needed extra weight to shore up her defences against any man before, and she wasn't too proud of the fact that she was prepared to use Martin as a sort of ballast. It was weak of her, but necessary, and it wouldn't hurt Martin. Martin's affections were shallow, which was why he could flit from her to Tara and back again to her. Next week he would probably have his sights set on some other girl. He was too much of a lightweight to be deeply hurt.

It occurred to her that she hadn't realised this before because most of the young men of her acquaintance were of the same calibre, until she met David. Would it always be like this from now on? Would she measure every man she met against David, and find him lacking, because David's strength of character was unique?

She wished that Martin could have been installed in Larkspur Cottage before her parents returned from their shopping expedition, and then she could have presented him as a fait accompli. As it was, she had to explain to her mother that Martin would be arriving shortly.

Her mother's smile disappeared. She said

gravely: 'I hope you know what you are doing, Jan.' Unexpectedly she added, 'Don't make a proud man humble himself too much.'

What did her mother mean? A proud man. She couldn't be referring to Martin.

'I'm not playing one off against the other, if that's what you mean.'

'That's the last thought I would entertain in connection with you, Jan. Such a devious ploy wouldn't enter your head, and even if it did, your 'one and only' complex wouldn't let you give a very convincing performance. You have a lot of praiseworthy characteristics, Jan, many of them inherited from your Grandmother Ashton, but I wish she hadn't passed her inflexible outlook on to you. You would save yourself a lot of trouble if your reasoning could be a bit more elastic.'

Her mother hadn't spoken frivolously. There was thought and meaning behind her words, but Jan couldn't come up with a sensible interpretation.

'He loves you, Jan. Can't you see?'

'Who, Martin?'

'Not Martin. He only loves himself.'

Who then? David? Did he? Could he? Her mother was biased. She couldn't see how anyone could not love her darling daughter.

She sighed, and put her mind back to the problem of where to sleep Martin. In normal circumstances she would have given him the sofa in the living room, but that would be lumpy comfort for a man with a broken arm. Poor Martin. He never could stand pain and he'd always yelled before he was hurt. As a little boy his mouth had turned down when things weren't going exactly his way, and he hadn't altered in this respect. Only one thing for it, he would have to have her room and she would have to double up with Stephanie. Stephanie's bed wasn't very big, but luckily neither was she or Stephanie.

'You can help me change the sheets and pillowcases on my bed for Martin,' she informed the little girl.

Normally, Stephanie loved to 'help'. It was most unlike her to answer listlessly, 'All right.'

'Don't you want me in your bed?' Jan asked. 'I don't kick.'

Stephanie summoned up a giggle. 'I do. Sometimes I kick Tatty Bear right out of bed.'

'Poor Tatty Bear,' said Jan.

If she hadn't been so wrapped up in her own affairs she would have spotted Stephanie's flushed cheeks and waxy pallor, and taken more notice of her apathy. As it was, Stephanie's lethargic mood went unheeded as she concentrated her attentions on the other invalid.

He arrived in a very sorry-for-himself state of mind. The train had arrived late and instead of trying to make up the time it had crawled from station to station at a tediously slow pace. He had been lumbered with a talkative woman, and the child on the seat behind him had divided his time between kicking Martin's seat and wiping his toffee-sticky hands round the back of his neck. He couldn't shave properly, tie a tie or a shoelace, hence the fact that he was wearing an open-necked shirt and casual slip-on shoes, both of which he deplored. But above all he was bored, bored, bored! And he hoped Jan had got a good evening lined up for him.

The early night that Jan had thought Martin would appreciate was never proposed. She was still wildly searching her brain for inspiration when her mother said: 'Why don't you put the steak back in the fridge, Jan, borrow your father's car, and take Martin out for a meal? I will be happy to babysit.'

In default of a better idea, Jan said: 'Yes. When David gets home from work I'll ask him if he can recommend a good place. You didn't tell me how the shopping expedition went. Did you spend up?'

'Well. Let's say I had a pretty good try.'

Her mouth went very smug. Jan was still probing the mystery when Martin said: 'Are you having a party?'

'A party?' Jan questioned, looking perplexed.

'Don't be so stupid,' Martin said with a touch of irritation. 'I know twenty-one isn't the official coming of age, but it's always good for a celebration.'

Twenty-one! On Sunday, which was the day

after tomorrow, it was her birthday. Her twenty-first birthday. How could she have forgotten that?

'You always were a blab-mouth, Martin Groves,' her mother said. 'Did you have to make it so obvious that we've been to Harrogate to shop for Jan's present?' Turning to her daughter she said: 'It wasn't last minute, honestly. Your main present's been wrapped for ages. I wanted something extra for you.'

'I'd completely forgotten my birthday,' Jan said stupidly.

'At your age, dear?' her mother said drily.

'Did you get something nice?' Martin asked, a little peevishly because he hadn't taken kindly to Muriel Ashton's chiding tone.

'Something very nice. But you are not going to wheedle it out of me just what.' She stood up and held her hand out towards Stephanie. 'Would you like me to take you to bed, pet?'

Stephanie went without demur and Jan set the table for her parents and David.

Muriel Ashton came back downstairs. 'David not here yet?'

'No. He does have a tendency to forget time when he's involved in something,' Jan admitted, 'but it's unlike him to be this late, and he's made a special point of being on time since you've been here, so as not to hold up the evening meal.'

'As far as I'm concerned it's not going to be held up much longer. I'm hungry. If he doesn't show up soon, he'll be eating alone.'

Before Jan could comment, Martin popped his head round the door. 'Anybody any good at tying ties? I refuse to have a night on the town wearing an open-necked shirt.'

'Better let me,' Jan heard her father say, which was as well because Martin had quibbled constantly from the moment he arrived. If she got her hands on his tie she might just be tempted to strangle him with it.

'Hope the local scene is lively, Jan,' Martin said in all innocence.

'You've got to be joking. There isn't one.'

'Surely we can let down the drawbridge and get out? Where do you go? You must have been somewhere.'

'Yes, I have. Danielle's Den. Thanks for reminding me. We'll go there. If you'll excuse me, I'll go up and get ready.'

She put on the same dress she had worn on the previous two occasions she had visited Danielle's Den. The thought glanced across her mind that she really must treat herself to a new dress, but her appearance wasn't her main preoccupation. If David still hadn't arrived home when she got downstairs, she wondered if she dare phone Linda whose husband, Hugh, worked with David, to ask her if Hugh had got home yet. She decided against it. It would sound too much like fussing. Anyway, David must surely have turned up by now.

He hadn't.

Her father handed over his car keys. 'Drive carefully, Jan.'

He always said that, even though he had told her countless times that he had every confidence in her as a driver.

'I will.' Turning to her mother she said: 'If anything crops up, you know where to find me. The number of Danielle's Den will be in the phone book.'

'Of course. Off you go and have a good time.'

'We shall certainly do that,' Martin averred, his good humour restored now that they were on the move. 'Danielle's Den. Intriguing sort of name. Tell me about it.'

Jan filled him in on the way, mentioning that Danielle was a friend of David's, but was careful to say nothing of Danielle's unhappy past.

'Hey, this looks all right to me,' Martin said as they plunged into the dimly lit room where a spotlight picked out Danielle who was seated at her usual place at the piano. His eyes were glued on Danielle.

Jan smiled. 'Why don't you say what you mean, and that is *she* looks all right?'

His grin was sheepish. 'Well she does. She's a stunner. You said she was a friend of your boss. Is she a special friend?'

'Very special,' Jan replied without hesitation.

'Wedding bells in the offing?'

'No, it's not that sort of friendship. Can't a man and a woman want to share each other's company because they like each other? Does physical attraction have to come into it?'

She hadn't realised how terse she sounded until Martin's hand shot up to fend off an imaginary blow. 'Sorry I spoke. I honestly had no idea or I would have been more tactful.'

'What on earth do you mean?'

'Come off it, Jan. Does David know how you feel about him? And remember it's me you are talking to and prevarication can serve no useful purpose.'

Her haughtiness dropped away. She sighed. 'David doesn't know. And he mustn't.'

'Don't look at me like that. I've never grassed in my life. I'm curious to know why you invited me up, though.'

'Because you'd broken your arm and you could do with a bit of pampering.'

'That's fine. But if you had any idea in that crazy head of yours that I look anything remotely like decoy material, forget it and find yourself another sitting duck.'

'A sitting duck, you? Never! You're never still enough, for one thing. Now if you'd said lame duck . . .'

'Ha! Very funny!' His handsome head lifted. 'Your little friend has stopped playing. Do you think you can persuade her to come and sit with us?'

'I don't think that will be necessary. I rather

imagine she'll come anyway.'

Jan was right. Even as she spoke she saw Danielle making her way through the tables towards them. Martin had set her thinking. David and Danielle. They would be so right for each other. Even their names were compatible. Their roots were deeply linked in sympathy. They liked what they knew about each other. How long before they found out they simply liked each other and decided to take it from there?

'Hello, Jan.' By this time Danielle had reached their table. The French girl pulled a chair forward for herself and sat down.

Martin, who had risen as Danielle approached, sat down also. 'You play beautifully.'

He wasn't wasting any time in getting into action, Jan noticed. He was seducing her with his eyes.

'No, I'm merely adequate.' Danielle's gaze lowered in provocative awareness. Or was there a quirk to her mouth that suggested to Jan it might be to conceal suppressed laughter. It was more likely for a sophisticated girl such as Danielle to have her mouth lifted in amusement than have her head turned by Martin's unsubtle approach.

'I've known Martin since I was a little girl, and he's quite harmless,' Jan said as a preliminary to the introduction.

'No, I'm not,' Martin defended himself

206

stoutly. 'Not completely armless anyway. I can still bring impudent little girls to heel with my remaining good arm.'

'I noticed you'd been in the wars. What exactly happened?' Danielle enquired compassionately.

Martin's eyes, which had no yearning to venture from Danielle's face, were still doing their witchcraft. A hint of mischief crept into their blue depths. 'I went to the defence of a poor little old lady who was being set upon by a gang of thugs. They had designs on the case she was carrying. They had it on good authority it was full of . . .'

'Yes?' Danielle leaned forward expectantly.

'. . . fruit and nut chocolate bars.'

'The only fruit and nut case is you. No, correction. I am also, for believing you. Now that I've got your measure, I won't be taken in again. You might have warned me, Jan, that your friend was a joker.'

'I *would* be a candidate for protective care if I told you how I really came to break my arm.'

Jan noticed that Martin's fun-talk had lightened the shadows in Danielle's eyes. The crying sadness behind her smile was less apparent than it had been when Jan had sat across a table from her with David.

Almost on cue, as if she had followed the direction of her thoughts, Danielle turned to Jan. 'Where is David? Is he following on?'

'David isn't coming this evening. I don't

know where he is. He hadn't got home from work when we set off.'

'Don't look so distraught, *chérie*. When you and David are married and he tells you he has had to work late, you can be sure it will not be a blind to cover up other activities.'

'I must set you right, Danielle. David and I are not going to be married.'

'No? I'm sorry to question your wisdom, my little friend, but are you not being silly? What is it you English say, are you not cutting off your nose to spite your face?'

'On the contrary. I'm saving face by cutting off my nose.' It wasn't her nose she was cutting off, it was her heart she was cutting out. 'I'm trying to be sensible.'

'That is something I do not know about. I have never been sensible in my life, and at my age . . .'

'Which is?' Martin cut in impertinently.

'I would not dream of telling you that,' Danielle said with a twinkle in her eye. 'But the first figure is a two. Have you noticed how long my fingers are? When I play the piano I can span an octave. The second figure is more than I can span with my fingers.'

There are eight notes in an octave. That made Danielle twenty-nine. Jan didn't know how old David was, but she thought he could claim a year, possibly two, more than that.

'I thought you said David wasn't coming this evening?' Danielle said.

'He isn't.'

'Then his ghost walks, or he has a double, because here he is.'

Jan turned her head, and there indeed was David, glowering down at her.

'What is it, David? I thought something must have happened when you didn't come home from work at your usual time.'

'Oh that. It's nothing to do with that. I'm afraid I got absorbed in what I was doing and forgot the time. I'm sorry to have thrown the meal arrangements to pot.'

'You haven't eaten, David? No? That's splendid. You must have a meal here. And do please sit down,' Danielle further instructed. 'You are so tall. I'm getting a crick in my neck with having to look all that way up at you.'

'I'll sit down for a moment, but I won't stay for a meal. I'm sorry to interrupt your evening, Jan, but I've come to take you home.'

Now that her anxiety had calmed, now that she saw he was fit and well and hadn't met with an accident, she became intensely annoyed. How dare he calmly walk in here and order her home? Her mother had obviously told him about Martin, and just as obviously it was not to his liking. His high-handedness roused her ire.

'I'm not going home. I'm not a child to be ordered about, and I'm enjoying myself too much to be dragged home because of some stupid whim of yours. I think you know Martin by name,' she said too sweetly, 'although I don't believe the two of you have actually met.'

Paying her out in her own coin, because he was alert to how her mind was working, he turned to address Martin. 'We've not actually met, but I do recall seeing you before.'

Curiosity surely insisted that Martin ask where. He must have sensed some innuendo because Jan felt herself the victim of his puzzled gaze, although he said nothing. She silently thanked him for not pursuing the issue. She remembered well where David had seen Martin before.

Like a dog with a bone, David said with irritating persistence: 'On that occasion, too, I came to take Jan back.'

It was after David had dismissed her and sent her home, because he considered her unsuitable for the job of looking after Stephanie, and altogether too indiscreet. But Stephanie had thought differently, and David had been forced to follow her and bring her back. His timing had been most unfortunate. Martin had made a pass at her, and David had been there at the crucial moment and had witnessed the scene through the uncurtained window.

'You seem to make a habit of coming after Jan to take her back,' Martin said, matching David's dryness as in turn each man summed up the other's potential.

'Unfortunately it would appear so,' David

admitted.

Jan had taken it for granted that David, with his astute judgement, would sum Martin up and find him wanting. It came to her that this was not so. David was in a livid temper and as usual the heat of his anger was crusted in ice. If it hadn't been such a ridiculous notion she would have thought he was jealous of Martin.

He said: 'There will be other opportunities for you to have entertaining evenings out in—' His eyes were mocking, but whatever they mocked it was not her taste in men— 'congenial company. Occasions that do not infringe on your conscience or your duty. Right now, I must ask you to put your mind to these mundane moral issues, even if it means forgoing your own pleasure.'

Even as she was silently applauding Martin for setting himself up as a worthy opponent, she was inwardly quaking. 'I don't know what you mean. My duty to whom? What moral issue? My conscience is perfectly clear.'

'Then all I can say is, you have a very convenient conscience if it allows you to embark on an evening of revelry leaving a sick child in the care of . . .'

'Now wait a minute,' Danielle intervened on her behalf. 'You can't speak to Jan like that.'

'If you'd let him finish, Danielle, he could only say that I left Stephanie in the care of a level-headed, capable adult. My mother. Is that not so, David? And what do you mean by a sick child? Stephanie was perfectly well when I left.'

But was she? The things that Jan hadn't properly registered with her eye, but which her brain had stored up for later recollection, flooded into her awareness. Stephanie's funny colour, the rose points in the cheeks of an otherwise pale little face. Her lack of bounce and fun which amounted to listlessness.

'I'll grant that your mother is a very capable woman,considerably more so than you are. But tell that to Stephanie, not to me. I'll give you the benefit of the doubt that you missed the signs and didn't deliberately walk out, knowing that she was sickening for something. Your mother is most insistent that her temperature flared up after you'd gone, but the fact remains that Stephanie has got herself worked up into a state because you aren't there. She isn't going to settle down until you come. Will you do so voluntarily, or must I take you by force. Make no mistake, you're coming even if I have to drag you every step of the way by the roots of your hair.'

'If you'd told me that Stephanie was ill in the first place, there would have been no argument,' Jan flung at him, rising to her feet. 'I'm sorry, Martin—' Twisting round to look at him—'but you see we must go.'

Martin didn't see. 'Must we? Kids are up and down all the time. Surely you know that. And as you've just said, she's in your mother's excellent hands. I don't see what you can do if you go back. It's a ridiculous idea.'

It was evident that Martin wasn't going to have his fun curtailed. He was digging in his heels to stay.

With ill-concealed impatience, so perhaps she could appreciate how David felt, she said: 'If you could drive, Martin, I'd go home with David and leave Dad's car for you to make your own way in your own time. But you can't drive with that arm, so you have no choice but to come with me.'

'May I make a suggestion,' Danielle said, taking the role of mediator upon herself. 'If Martin wants to stay, I'll drive him back. Or, better still, he could shack up for the night with Tom, my manager. He's got a spare room in his flat, and I know he'd willingly put Martin up if I asked him. What do you think, Martin?'

Martin thought it was a splendid idea, and Jan was free to go with David.

In the car park David said: 'You found your way here all right, so presumably you know the way back?'

'Yes,' she replied meekly.

The sarcastic inflection dropped from his voice. 'You drive first, and I'll follow to keep an eye on you. I'm sorry for spoiling your evening,' he added unexpectedly.

'You haven't really,' Jan admitted. 'And you've made Martin's. Is Martin at all like Stephen?'

'Strange that you should ask that, but yes. He is the same character type. What put you on to that?'

'Danielle's interest in Martin, I suppose. People are invariably attracted to the same type of person, don't you agree?'

'No I don't. You're talking utter rubbish. If it's been an unhappy experience, anybody with a grain of sense will be wary of seeking happiness with the same type.'

Jan opened her mouth to reply, but shut it again with her thoughts unvoiced.

They got into their respective cars and she led off on the homeward journey.

Sense doesn't, or shouldn't, come into it. Love *is*. It's not something that can be coolly and sensibly sought out.

If only David had come looking for her, threatening to drag her back by the roots of her hair because he loved her and couldn't live another moment without her, and couldn't bear the thought of her being out with another man. And not because Stephanie was ill and fretfully crying out for her. This would always be the way of it, which is why she must not weaken in her resolution to go away.

How unrealistic and absurd of her to imagine, even for a brief moment, that David cared enough to be jealous because she was with Martin.

CHAPTER EIGHT

Martin had been right in one respect. Children are up and down. By the time they arrived at Larkspur Cottage, Stephanie's fluctuating temperature had dropped to a safe level and she was sleeping normally.

Jan's mother met them at the door with a rueful smile. 'Sorry I panicked. The child is undoubtedly cooking something up and it would be a wise precaution to have the doctor to her in the morning, but I shouldn't have sent you out again, David, when you'd only just come in from work, and also spoil your evening, Jan.'

'You know it's all right by me, Mum. I'd rather be called back on a dozen false alarms than have Stephanie really poorly.'

'Yes, of course.' Briskly fastening on her apron she said: 'I'll get you something to eat now, David.'

'I don't really want anything, thank you, Muriel. I'm not hungry.'

'What's that got to do with it? If I say you eat, my boy, then you eat.' She looked up at him, and as she was even smaller than Jan, she had a considerable way to look. 'A big frame like yours needs filling.'

It was comical to see her mother's diminutive figure standing up to David's tallness. He could have picked her up and moved her aside quite easily with one hand. As it was he succumbed to her bossy tone, sent her a shy smile and dropped obediently into the chair she had set for him at the table.

Jan, whose own appetite had been whipped away by her concern for Stephanie, could sympathise. At the same time she smiled inwardly because someone could get the better of him. Not for long did she smile, though.

'She didn't get round to eating either,' David said treacherously, and to Jan's dismay a second knife and fork clattered on to the table.

Jan glowered at him, attempted to say something, but caught his absurd, little-boy look before she could channel her pique into words, found it was all too much for her, and burst into reluctant laughter.

*   *   *

When it came to bedtime, Jan didn't know which room to head for. If Martin wasn't going to use her room, she might as well. But what if Martin changed his mind, or for some reason Tom, Danielle's manager, couldn't put him up for the night and he came back to Larkspur Cottage? Rather than risk the problem that would create, Jan decided to slip in with Stephanie. She managed this with minimal disturbance. Stephanie stirred, flung out her

216

arm, but remained asleep. Her edge-of-the-bed position was not the most comfortable perch Jan could imagine, but she was very tired, quite drained, and eventually she slept.

A crash awakened her. She had no idea what it was. Something . . . somebody . . . moving about downstairs. It had sounded more like a splintering breaking crash, rather than the resounding thud of a chair being knocked over.

She was on the point of getting out of bed to investigate, not too urgently because her first theory of burglars had been replaced by the thought that after all Martin must have decided to come back, when the bedroom door opened.

As she raised up in the dark, a gentle hand on her shoulder persuaded her to lie down again.

'Hush, darling. I'm sorry to have disturbed you. I was only checking that you were all right.'

Jan's alerted senses identified the tall figure, even though it was too dark to see, and her heart missed a beat at being called darling, even though the cherished endearment had come to her by courtesy of false pretences. Her heart almost stopped altogether, as David's lips lightly brushed her forehead. 'You're cool, anyway.'

She could tell by the laughing inflection in his voice that the game was up, because now

David had recognised her.

Cool was something she was not.

'We'll have to stop meeting like this,' he said humorously.

'David, I . . .'

'Jan, if ever you are in this sort of situation again, do you mind speaking up a bit sooner. At first I did think you were Stephanie. I might just have slid in beside you for a cuddle.'

'Such talk. Will you please go before you wake her up.'

'Is she all right?' His eyes would now be more accustomed to the gloom, and he appeared to look over her at the hump under the bedclothes that was Stephanie.

'She's fine. Now go.'

'If she's fine, what are you doing here?'

'I'm trying to get some sleep. I know that's not the answer you want. I'll explain fully tomorrow. Just before you go, what was that noise?'

'What noise?'

'A sort of crashing, splintering sort of noise.'

'It was just that. A crashing, splintering sort of noise. I accidentally knocked over Mrs. Weaver's blue vase, and it's now in pieces on the floor.'

Jan burst into tears.

'But you didn't like it. It was hideous. I've done you a favour.'

Jan couldn't say that it had nothing to do with the vase. That it was hideous, and she had never liked it, and that in breaking it he had done her a favour. If she'd said that she would have had to tell him why she was crying, and she couldn't tell him that because she didn't know. She didn't know that her emotions were in such a tight knot that the most trivial thing was capable of acting as catalyst and activating the tears.

'Tomorrow is Saturday. I don't have to go to work. I'll go out and buy you another blue vase, every bit as hideous.'

'Goodnight, David.'

She thought he would never go, but eventually he went.

* * *

Doctor Ives said that Stephanie had picked up a virus. The root cause was undoubtedly Stephanie's troublesome tonsils which, unless a vast improvement took place, would have to come out.

The kindly doctor went. Muriel Ashton observed the mischievous-eyed patient.

She said: 'This little madam is enjoying the extra bit of fuss and attention.'

Stephanie had certainly picked up. Jan was kept on the trot meeting Stephanie's endless chant of, 'Fetch me a book . . . a drink . . . sweeties.' She was more than a little relieved when her mother called up the stairs: 'Jan. Aren't you supposed to be going shopping?'

219

'I want to come shopping with you,' Stephanie promptly announced.

'Sorry, poppet, it's just not on. You've got to stay in bed and get better for my birthday tomorrow. I don't want a poorly little girl spoiling my birthday, now do I?'

Stephanie considered. 'Will you have a birthday cake?'

Jan said confidentially: 'At this very moment my mother is baking a cake. I have my suspicions that it just might turn out to be a birthday cake.'

'With icing and candles?'

'Of course. It wouldn't be a birthday cake without icing and candles.'

'How many candles will it have?'

'Lots and lots.'

'A hundred?'

From the doorway, David teased: 'Jan's getting to be quite an old lady now, but not that old. How many candles will there be, Jan?' Knowing laughter lurked in his dark eyes, even though his face was serious.

The devil, he knew!

One of her parents must have blabbed on her. The likeliest candidate was her mother because she had the liveliest tongue.

'Twenty-one,' she admitted on a lilting laugh, because she seemed to have caught his mood. 'As if you didn't know.'

He didn't admit that he did, but neither did he offer a denial. 'I'll walk down to the village with you,' he said. 'I've some shopping to do myself.'

* * *

Walking down towards the jumble of stone buildings in its vale setting, with the sun warm on their faces and the encircling hills wearing identical Summer-green hats and amiably sharing the twisting ribbon road that tied up with the path Jan and David were walking on, it was peace personified. More than that, this haven that Jan was contemplating leaving was indisputably her spiritual home. In the gloomily appraised future, wherever her body might take up residence, her thoughts would for ever remain here.

With painful decision she said: 'There is something I must tell you, David, and now is as good a time as any. I want you to find someone else to look after Stephanie. I had planned to go home with my parents when they leave, but I've since come round to thinking that it wouldn't be fair to you. I won't leave you in the lurch, but I want you to make an all out effort to find someone to replace me.'

'I don't rightly see how I can let you go, Jan,' he said, sounding superbly casual.

'Nobody is indispensable. You'll get somebody as good as, or better, than me,' she affirmed. 'See you.' And she shot into Alice Spink's general store.

She was glad it was a busy Saturday morning. When it got round to her turn to be served, she could give her order in a reasonably composed voice.

Alice Spink slammed the provisions on the counter, totting them up in her head as she went along, and Jan transferred them to her capacious shopping bag.

'I'm sorry I haven't the exact amount,' Jan said, proffering some notes.

'That's all right, dear. I'm not short.' Alice Spink resorted to her old trick of not handing over the change. When change is given the customer is free to make a quick getaway. When change is withheld, the loquacious proprietress had a captive audience. This time it was with definite purpose and not gossipy intent. 'Remember when you first came here asking for all manner of out of the ordinary commodities, and I said we only stocked the basics because we'd no call for the others. Well my Diane, she's a bright girl, said that perhaps we'd no call for the others because we didn't stock them. So on Thursday when the traveller called, I went a bit mad and put an order in. All being well it should be delivered on Tuesday, which is the regular delivery day. So now you won't have to go trailing all the way into Didsford for this type of thing.'

It was worded as a consideration, but it sounded suspiciously like a command. Jan had only been to Didsford the once, and that was to buy the plaque for The Retreat. It had duly arrived and looked rather splendid on the door of David's quarters. While she was in Didsford she had made a point of buying in one or two delicacies which were not obtainable from the village shop. Had one of Alice Spink's spies spotted her and reported back, and was she having her hands slapped for disobeying the unwritten law to trade locally?

'It's kind of you to let me know and I appreciate it, but I won't be doing my shopping here much longer.'

'Oh!' said Alice Spink, visibly rising on her dignity.

'Oh, nothing wrong. Just the reverse. You've spoilt me for town shopping. But you see, I'm planning to leave quite soon. I'll be off the moment Mr. Spedding finds a replacement to look after Stephanie.'

'I'm not surprised at that,' said Alice Spink putting on a sympathetic face. 'The surprise is that a sweet young girl such as yourself has stood that man for so long.'

'What do you mean, Mrs. Spink?'

'Well, it stands to reason that you only stayed on this long for the little girl's sake. And don't misunderstand me because we all admire you for it. No blame's been put on you for tolerating the likes of him. I mean, the facts speak for themselves. He hasn't a drop of common decency in his body.'

This gossip wasn't new. Jan had heard it all

before, but she hadn't known David then. Just as Alice Spink and the ladies who had come in after Jan and were waiting their turn, didn't know David. She could tell by their expressions that they were all in agreement with Alice Spink.

Turning to the assembly at large, shrivelling up every last one of them with the heat of her anger, she let rip. 'You couldn't be more wrong. Just as I've been wrong. Not only about David Spedding, but about you. I looked upon your endless gossiping as a bit of harmless nosiness to compensate for the narrow lives you lead. But you are nothing but a bunch of spiteful old biddies. If you carry on voicing such misinformed, malicious rubbish, you could just find yourself tangling with the law. Except that David Spedding is too kind and caring to put you through the distress that your destructive tongues have caused him. He is the kindest, the most fair-minded, just and noble person I've ever met or am ever likely to meet.'

Alice Spink took a step back, dumbfoundedly gathering her wits. Shocked breaths were drawn all round Jan, but it was left to Alice Spink to retaliate.

She was obviously going to do it in style. Never short of words for long, she said with dignity and—to Jan's intense surprise—with approval: 'Bravo, my girl. I didn't know you had that much explosion in you. My husband has always said that I'm a bit too handy at giving out the stick, but I don't yelp when it's turned back on me. Most of what I've said has been related to me by someone else, and I freely admit that I prefer to rely on my own observations. The moment I set eyes on you I figured you out to be a no-nonsense girl with a good head on your young shoulders. You've given me no cause to modify that first snap judgement. Many a stronger person would have quailed at what you've had to tackle. We all admired Annabel Spedding for her courage, but on the quiet we had a sneaking suspicion that she put you through it. And there's none more ashamed than me for letting you get on with it, with never a complaint or a grumble passing your lips, although you must have been hard pressed at times. I reckon we had to blacken somebody else's character to make ours look white. I admit that without a lot of pride, I can tell you.'

'But you were the first to offer help, Mrs. Spink,' Jan protested.

'Aye, that's as may be. But I didn't do much pressing when it was turned down. As far as David Spedding is concerned, you're nobody's fool, my girl, and I reckon if anybody's got his measure, it's you. It's not easy to change tune mid air. If you've been one of the crows it's a bit difficult to start singing like a canary, so you'll just have to bide with me for a while. You could perhaps tell me one thing. If he's as

225

fine and honourable as you make out, how come he didn't show up for her funeral?'

'I don't know,' Jan said, the wind taken out of her sails by Alice Spink's deep dip into her own sense of justice. 'One thing I do know. There will be a perfectly valid reason why he didn't come.'

She held out her hand for the change, turned, and walked out of the shop and smack into David. As the door had been propped open, as it usually was on busy shopping days, he must have heard every word.

'Exchange is no robbery,' he said taking the full shopping bag from her and entrusting into her hands an oblong box bearing the name Studio Potteries. 'I couldn't exactly replace the vase I broke.'

In entranced stupefaction she said: 'Somebody loves me. Praise heaven you couldn't find an exact copy. You . . . er . . . heard?'

'The whole village heard. Thank you for defending me. You were right, of course. I would have paid my last respects had it been possible. I couldn't attend the funeral because at the time I was in quarantine.'

'Why didn't you say, instead of letting everybody think the worst of you?'

'Not everybody. Those in the know would appreciate without explanation that I was forcibly prevented. Those who didn't know would have made too much out of it. It was

226

more or less a routine precaution taken after a particular form of experimental work. But to the layman the word quarantine has an awesome ring. It could have started a national scare.'

'That's what Linda was trying to tell me that time, when you shut her up.'

'It's better for people not to know certain things.'

'I'm not people. I'm me.'

'Yes, but I didn't know you then.'

'Does your work often put you at risk?'

'No, of course not.'

She sighed. 'It was silly of me to ask that, because you wouldn't tell me if it did.'

Of one accord they'd stopped walking. His free hand turned her chin. 'You're marvellous, Jan. No wonder I love you.'

She gulped. 'Would you mind repeating that?'

'I love you,' he said simply and with utter sincerity.

Tears melted her vision. She thought she must have misheard him first time. The confirmation was so unexpected that she almost dropped the replacement piece of pottery. 'Of all the places to tell me.'

'I've tried to play the gentleman's waiting game to give you chance to sort out your feelings, not always too successfully because I've come to the conclusion that it's the cad who has the most fun. Come to me soon, Jan.

The difference in our ages isn't going to afford you protection for much longer, because I'm finding it harder to keep away from you. Do you realise that I am ten years older than you are? You led me to believe it was a mere six years, but a comment of your father's enlarged the gap.'

'My father told you? When? I thought it was my mother who gave me away.'

'It was when I had dismissed you and then come to fetch you back. Do you remember that talk your father had with me? He was slightly uneasy about the set-up. He said you were ill-prepared for the hazards that beset young girls, that your impetuosity afforded nil protection, while your trusting nature put you at especially grave risk. He told me I must not amuse myself with you, only he put it a bit stronger than that.'

'Oh, he couldn't have,' Jan said, flushing with embarrassment. 'I don't know what I'm going to do with him. It's time he got out of his Victorian parlour.'

'I liked his bluntness and his concern.'

'I'm wondering what you said to Dad.'

'I think I reassured him. I told him I had only put you to bed the once.'

'You didn't!'

'Didn't tell him? Or didn't put you to bed?'

'I was ill. Somebody had to put me to bed. You were the only person there at first, apart from Stephanie, until you got Linda to come.

A chivalrous man would have skipped over that little episode.'

'Chivalry is dull.'

Her sense of the absurd came to her rescue and she saw a way of paying him back. 'You looked after me so solicitously. Not that I remember all that much in my semi-delirious state.' She tried to keep a straight face as she delivered her punch line. 'I thought you were my father.'

'I tried that one too. Unfortunately it didn't work for me. I couldn't think of you as my daughter. I had to get Linda in, quick.'

'Dad looked after me one time when my grandmother was very ill and my mother, like any loving daughter-in-law would, went to nurse her. He couldn't manage the bows and those fiddly little pearl buttons either.'

'So what chance had I, an inexperienced boy,' he said with a very straight face. On a more serious note he said: 'What about your grandmother?'

'She made a marvellous recovery and is fighting fit. She'll outlive us all.'

'I don't like the emphasis you put on the word fighting. Don't say I've got another hot-headed Ashton to deal with?'

'Didn't I tell you? Grandmother Ashton is the original fire-eating Ashton. I am but the pale copy.' But there was nothing soft-hued about her joy. It showed in the sparkling exultation of her smile and the glimpse of heaven magically brightening her eyes. 'My grandmother will adore you. When we get back to the cottage, may I phone and tell her about us?' With a shaky laugh she said: 'Tell me about us, David. I can't seem to take it in.'

'I love you. Fix that very firmly in your mind, my darling.'

'Why? Aren't you going to tell me again?'

'Only every day for the rest of my life. You are my life, my joy, my happiness. I wish I could just pick you up and run off with you. Only I think it will please your parents if we wait to make a slight detour by way of the church.'

'Yes, I'm inclined to agree with you.'

'That makes a most pleasant change,' he teased gently. 'Will they mind having Stephanie dumped on them? I'd like to have you to myself at least for the honeymoon.'

The thought of going on a honeymoon with David almost took her breath away. The only voice at her command was a very insubstantial thing as she replied: 'They'll enjoy having Stephanie, I know. She makes them feel young.'

'That's odd. She puts years on me. Most couples can count on a little time entirely to themselves before they start a family. All we can manage is two weeks before we come home to our ready-made daughter. Do you feel cheated, Jan?'

She considered for a moment and then said:

'I would dearly love to have some growing-together time just with you, but I wouldn't forfeit Stephanie for it. I love her for herself and she couldn't feel more mine if I'd given birth to her. And I love her for bringing us together. If there hadn't been a Stephanie to care for, I would have locked up Larkspur Cottage, left the key with the solicitor, and had no cause to meet you. It's so frightening it doesn't bear thinking about.'

Blatantly disregarding the fact that they were on a public highway, David pulled her to him and cradled her head against his chest. 'Don't ever again entertain such a possibility. Never to have met you. Never to have known real happiness, real joy, real fun.'

He held her for a moment, as though he was comforting away that horrible thought. Jan remained very still, feeling very secure.

He began to speak again. 'I'm no sinner, but then again I'm no saint, and I thank God for caring enough about me to bring someone as wonderful as you into my life. I'm going to devote myself to making you happy. We'll have a marvellous marriage, Jan, I promise. We'll make a good home for Stephanie. Happiness has a magic radiation and ours will brush off on her to make up for the bad start she had in life. And please don't feel too badly of me for not wanting to share our happiness with her from the very beginning. The plans have been passed for the conversion of the two cottages into one, and the builders are waiting for me to give the word for them to move in. They can get cracking while we are away on honeymoon, but the work can't possibly be completed in time, so when we return will you mind too much if we move into The Retreat?'

'I'll love it. We'll rename it The Haven.'

'If you go on like that, I'll be asking your parents to keep Stephanie on after the honeymoon, until the conversion of the two cottages is completed.'

To think, she once thought he only wanted to marry her because Stephanie needed a mother.

'I thought that when you asked me to marry you, it was because you'd decided to settle for second best.'

'Where did you get that dumb idea from?'

'From you. You said surely one taste of the bitter enchantment was enough, and next time wasn't it better to play safe rather than wait for a fever-pitch romance that might never happen again? I might have missed something out, but that was the essence of it. I knew you meant how you felt for Annabel.'

'Everything we have ever said to each other seems to have been shadowed by misunderstanding. I never loved Annabel that way. I made the common enough mistake of confusing fascination with love. I didn't know what it was like to love at fever-pitch, or at any pitch, until I met you. When I said what I did, I was referring to you and Martin.'

Now it was Jan's turn to look surprised. 'You can't be serious? There was never anything more than fondness between us.'

'My jealous streak is very pleased to hear it. It's not how it appeared to me that time I saw you together,' he said with a hint of reproof.

'That wasn't as it seemed. Martin was taking it out on me because of what another girl did to him. I let him get on with it because I thought it would help him to get the sense of injustice out of his system. He didn't overstep the mark. I would have stopped him if he had.'

'I was ready to stop him if he had. With my fist. I hope it helped Martin, because I can tell you this, it didn't do me much good. You've a lot to make up to me for.'

Smiling in shy delight at the prospect, Jan said: 'Oh I will make it up to you. I promise.'

*   *   *

It took quite a long time, but eventually they returned to the cottage.

Muriel Ashton took one look at their faces, changed colour, hugged Jan, spontaneously raised up to kiss David's cheek, and said: 'My darlings, I couldn't be more pleased.'

'We're getting married,' Jan said, even though it was a case of putting the announcement after the congratulations. Turning to David she said: 'You did say I could

233

phone Grandmother to tell her the news?'

No reply.

'David, will you please put your mother-in-law-to-be down and answer me.'

'You surely know you don't need my permission for anything. Of course, go ahead and phone. While you're about it, tell her to pack a suitcase because I'm fetching her. A grandmother is an important enough person to be at a combined birthday and engagement celebration.'

Jan let out a gasp of delighted surprise. 'But David, it's a round trip of four hundred miles.'

'So what? If you want to come with me I could use the company.'

'I wish I could. But I can't leave Mother to cope on her own.'

'There's nothing to cope with. Everything has been taken care of,' Muriel Ashton said decisively.

'How can it be?' Jan protested. 'If Grandmother is coming, there will be extra shopping and baking to do and . . .'

It got through slowly to Jan that David and her mother were exchanging knowing looks. And what were they setting up between them? she wondered.

'I'm sorry, David,' her mother said. 'You can't say I didn't try.'

'Thanks anyway, Muriel. For peace's sake, I suppose I must tell her.'

'Tell me what?' Jan demanded, wishing

these two conspiritors wouldn't talk to each other as if she wasn't there.

David said with loving indulgence: 'You are a difficult girl to spring a surprise on, Jan. Even if you stayed, you'd only get in the way, because I've booked a very efficient catering service to do the honours. One grandmother more or less won't make a lot of difference.'

With unaccustomed docility, Jan went to phone her grandmother to inform her of the arrangements.

*   *   *

And so it was that Jan woke up on her birthday morning under her grandmother's roof. It wasn't so much that Grandmother thought the double journey was too much for them to make in one day, but that she wanted to get to know David on home ground. Jan further observed, to her amusement and delight, that David was proving an adequate match and even capped her grandmother's shrewdness. He stood up magnificently to the matriarchal interrogation, and then adeptly set about turning the tables on her darling, indomitable grandmother by returning her long, appraising stare. He was wise enough to spice his look with approval.

Afterwards, Jan was proud to inform her grandmother: 'David thinks you are a very handsome woman.'

Her grandmother chuckled. 'And he let it show, the scoundrel.' The smile in the eyes that were so like Jan's, softened. 'A very kind scoundrel. Male admiration is a treat not often accorded to me these days. I get respect in plenty, but your David acknowledged that I was a woman first, a grandmother second. I am well aware of his game. If anybody was going to be undermined, it wasn't going to be him, the naughty boy. But that one I could forgive anything.'

'You mean I have your approval, Grandmother?'

'Bless you for being kind enough to want it. I approve wholeheartedly. In his hands you will be kindly protected, but never stifled, and boredom will be a stranger at your door. He will be firm with you, but indulgent. I know it's unfashionable among the young for the man to be the master, but despite the fact that I'm considered to be a firebrand, I'm old-fashioned enough to think that's the right way round. Equality doesn't always bring happiness. With your David you will know a contented heart, and you will have happiness in abundance.'

Muriel Ashton, in apprehension of Grandmother Ashton's reaction, breathed easier when the three of them walked in next day, and she saw that David and her mother-in-law were on remarkably cosy terms.

It was a truly wonderful combined birthday and engagement party. Linda and Hugh were the first to arrive. Martin and Danielle came shortly afterwards, wearing very smug smiles. Danielle was obviously finding Martin a pleasant distraction. Jan was pleased for them, with one small reservation. She hoped Martin wouldn't prove to be a distraction that Danielle could do without.

She told herself firmly that it wasn't her business, and anyway Danielle wasn't a slip of a girl to be deceived by the trickery and cajolery of an experienced charmer. She was a mature woman, well able to hold her own in Martin's subtle game. In turn, it was noticeable that Martin found Danielle a dangerously exciting prospect. It would be a stroke of luck for him if she also proved to be a settling influence.

Jan had unwrapped and delighted over all her presents. A new dress from her parents, which she wore for the occasion, plus, round her neck, an antique gold locket and chain, the result of their shopping expedition to Harrogate. From her grandmother she had received a deeply fringed Spanish shawl. Linda, with a bright twinkle in her eye, had given Jan a make-up case from her and Hugh that contained a dazzling rainbow collection of eyeshadows and lipsticks and mysterious potions in intriguing little pots.

'I know it's like launching the sales campaign after the deal has been clinched, Jan dear,' she said.

'That's the way I operate,' Jan had quipped back.

Who else would fall in love with a man before coming to terms with liking him?

A thoughtful touch of her mother's was to produce a pretty apron and peg bag for Stephanie to give to her. Besides the pottery vase, which in no way resembled the hideous one he'd broken and was exquisite in line and detail, David gave her a slim, leather-bound volume of poetry to cherish, and 'this'. 'This' turned out to be an emerald and diamond ring in a Victorian setting.

'It was my grandmother's. I thought perhaps you could wear it until we have time to shop around for one of your choice.'

She searched his face. 'But it *is* my choice. It's so perfect that it's spoilt me for any other. Please may I keep this?'

'I was hoping you would say that. I wish my grandmother could have lived to know and love you, Jan. Wearing her ring is the next best thing. I spotted a bracelet quite recently that was an incredibly good match. I'll buy it for you.'

'No, you mustn't. You've already spent too much money on me.'

'Don't deny me the joy of giving you things,

Jan. For the first time in my life I'm getting more back than I'm giving.'

'Oh my love,' she said.

The corner of the room they shared offered only the illusion of privacy. David picked up Grandmother Ashton's birthday shawl and wrapped it round her shoulders. 'Come on. We are taking a walk.'

'But David,' she protested shyly. 'Everyone will know why we're going out.'

His eyes twinkled darkly. 'I don't give a damn. Are you coming voluntarily? Or do I take you by force?'

Her heart fluttered at the thought of being taken by force. Of being dragged outside because he couldn't survive another moment without having physical contact with her. Every woman wants to be wanted. His desire appeased her inner woman's primeval instincts. Her longing for him rushed the blood to her cheeks.

'You wouldn't. Not with everyone watching.'

'No?' he challenged. 'Try me, if you dare. Bearing in mind that your mother will approve. As I recall it, she once said that caveman tactics were underestimated by today's male. I never did get round to putting her theory to the test.'

'You've made your point.' She had savoured the anticipation to the full. She would delay no longer. 'I'm coming.'

*   *   *

They walked until they were out of sight of the cottage and then, of one accord, they stopped. His arms came round her and she lifted her face up for the kiss his eyes had promised her.

The warm and tender flame, encircling two hearts in a love that would never die, had been sending out teasing sparks all evening. It leapt into passion as their lips met.